# PEOPLE
## WHO
### TALK TO
# STUFFED
### ANIMALS
## ARE NICE

# AO OMAE

**Translated by Emily Balistrieri**

HARPERVIA

*An Imprint of* HarperCollins*Publishers*

# PEOPLE WHO TALK TO STUFFED ANIMALS ARE NICE

stories

HarperCollins books may be purchased for educational, business, or sales promotional use. For information, please email the Special Markets Department at SPsales@harpercollins.com.

Originally published as *Nuigurumi to shaberu hito wa yasashii* in Japan in 2020 by Kawade Shobō Shinsha.

FIRST HARPERVIA EDITION PUBLISHED 2023

*Designed by Yvonne Chan*

Library of Congress Cataloging-in-Publication Data is available upon request.

ISBN 978-0-06-322721-7

23 24 25 26 27 LBC 5 4 3 2 1

# CONTENTS

# REALIZING
# FUN
# THINGS
# THROUGH
# WATER

A package arrived from Kimiko. It was a heavy cardboard box, and the delivery slip said "hyper-organization water." There were ten bottles and a letter inside.

*How have you been? Going over the plan for the ceremony the other day, it really sank in. Please talk to the waters in these bottles every day. The best time is on an empty stomach when you have fewer impurities. Please choose fun topics as often as possible. Supposedly, if each atom is happy, the ions mature and help keep you from getting cancer. This miracle water even makes you more passionate; it's so popular I could only buy one box, so I'm sending it to you, Hatsuoka—because you need to take good care of your body. And if your sister comes home, please have her drink some, too. Please pray to the waters that she'll come back. Talk to you soon.*

I took a picture of the letter and sent it to Hakozaki. *She's getting scammed . . .* I thought, but I didn't write it. I didn't want to comment about my soon-to-be mother-in-law and make things complicated.

My sister used to write a lot about "special" water, "magic" water, and so on, too. Before she disappeared, she wrote fake news part time.

I poured some water into a cup and smelled it before taking a drink. It seemed like regular mineral water to me. *Something fun, something fun.* Had anything fun happened lately? "Yesterday the giraffe at the zoo had a birthday," I told the water. "The weather was nice. The sunset was pretty. The temperature was just perfect. I bought a neat teapot at the craft market they were holding at the shrine. I had pear cake at a café and it was tasty."

Once I got going, there was no shortage of fun things to talk about. I realized that even little things in my daily life were fun. I couldn't stop talking and even found myself saying, "What was that about taking good care of my body? Did she mean . . . ? What a pain." Since I was talking to a thing that couldn't get hurt—not a person I did or didn't get along with, not even a person or a living thing at all—I could say whatever I wanted.

Maybe my lover is just someone I like better than other people. Because he's less scary compared to other people. More kind. Because he won't hurt me. That's how I felt, which is why I'd been dating Yuri Hakozaki. Maybe that was rude to him, but it was also possible he felt the same way.

We were at a hedgehog café when he said, "Let's get married." It was 2,500 yen an hour. The hedgehogs were all in a glass case, and when you picked out the one you wanted, a member of the staff would transfer it into a little basket. We chose a hedgehog named Kohaku. Hakozaki and I took pictures and videos of her and fed her the dead bugs you could purchase for an extra fee. He knew I didn't feel like marriage was that important, so I was able to imagine that the cute animals had relaxed him, and he simply said it because he felt happy.

"Okay," I said.

Really I wanted to say, *Okay, but let me think about it a little bit.* But that would have hurt his feelings, so I didn't. I prioritized that single moment when deciding my future.

I hated that I had felt better before he proposed. I was happy, but at the same time, I was already sick of the idea. Imagining all the obnoxious things that would happen in the future—meeting to discuss the ceremony, deciding what to do about our last name, dealing with relatives, being bluntly asked when we're having kids by people I know and people I've never met—wore me out.

While Hakozaki was in the bathroom, I searched for things like "marriage depression," "marriage pain in the neck," "marriage relatives annoying." There were lots of people feeling listless about marriage and guilty toward their partner like me. There was no end to them. That exhausted me even more. I liked Hakozaki, so you'd think I could be more genuinely happy. It was worth celebrating. If a friend of mine were getting married, I would have been happy. Imagining that feeling on our way home from the hedgehog café, I told Hakozaki, "I'm *sooo* happy." Like there was no going back. So I would be able to focus on the happiness mixed in with the neck pains.

"Really? Wow, I'm so glad to hear that," said Hakozaki. "I was nervous." Tears came out of his eyes.

"I'm the worst," I said to the water, remembering that day. I hadn't been able to tell anyone but the water. Out of some sense of consideration, I was incapable of tormenting myself in front of other people. It felt good to criticize and understand myself.

That same day, Hakozaki told his parents about the proposal and that I'd accepted. I had met them any number of times over the six years we'd been dating.

"It was nice out today, so I came all the way to Kyoto, but suddenly I just want to lie down. My back is bent, you know. My name's Kimiko. How about you? Oh, Hatsuoka, huh. Feel free to call me Kimi, dear."

That was what she told me the first time we met. We were

at the condo where Hakozaki was living alone. Hakozaki was at work, and when I woke up to the sound of her opening the door, I was practically naked. When I told him what happened, he said, "Yeah, she can be bizarrely friendly."

That was true. About once every six months, she would contact me: "I'm going to be in your neighborhood, so why don't we go get tea?" At first I thought she meant with Hakozaki, too, but it was only ever me and her.

I must have been a perfectly distanced other. All the gripes Kimiko had about her life that she couldn't tell her family, or her co-workers at her part-time job, or the people in her neighborhood, she one-sidedly blasted at me. Not that I minded. She treated me to delicious cake and tea, and I was happy to be able to help someone let off steam by simply nodding and *uh-huh*ing mechanically now and then.

It stressed me out that she hit Like on everything I posted on Facebook and other social media, but she never interfered with my life or my relationship with Hakozaki.

Still, that was only because I was Hakozaki's girlfriend, an outsider. When she got word of the engagement, she pinged me, "Hatsuoka, you're already thirty, aren't you? Why not quit your part-time job or whatever and live with Yuri?"

It aggravated me, but I got it. Just as I had been worrying about how I was getting married and my family would expand, Hakozaki and his mom were probably worried in the same way—their family was growing, too. I wondered why I had to quit my job just because we were getting married, but I think she meant well in her own way, so I didn't have the heart to push back.

*I'm sure things like this will happen more and more frequently. There will be expectations of me as a new family member. Same goes for Hakozaki.* I held off for a while on telling my parents about the engagement.

Even if we got married, there was no way I would quit my job or live with Hakozaki. It had only been two years since my sister disappeared. *I want to wait for my sister. I want to keep paying our rent.* I wasn't sure if I should say that to Kimiko or not. Instead, I didn't write anything and just messaged back a flustered cat face sticker.

Apparently Hakozaki and I were in the same club in college. I say "apparently" because back then we hadn't met yet.

It was a movie-watching club. We didn't have a clubroom, so we either had to rent something and go to someone's house or go to a movie theater. I joined for the same reasons most people join clubs: I wanted more friends; I wanted to connect with people who shared my interests.

But twenty days after I sent the email to join, the club went bankrupt. Apparently, a founding member two years above me learned they were sick, so the club misappropriated the entire budget for their surgery without telling anyone. The club president sent an email in the middle of the night with a long explanation and apology. The next day was the surgery. *I'm feeling so anxious and bad about the whole thing that I'm crying as I write this. Since I used the money without permission, I need to take responsibility and disband the club,* the email said.

*Dang, that's rough,* I thought. That was all. I'd never seen the face of the person who got sick. I had never met the president, either. I hadn't gotten to participate in the club at all. I had already paid the 3,000 yen to join, but it was only 3,000 yen.

As far as I know, no one made a fuss about the club dues or the disbanding. Twelve years ago, we didn't have social media like we have now, and I wasn't in the Mixi group, so I didn't hear anyone getting angry about it. Remembering that is a relief.

I met Hakozaki a year after I graduated, at a curry joint. Every Saturday night they screened a movie on the restaurant's second floor. I found a flier in my mailbox, thought I might like to meet some people, invited my sister, and went to watch a movie projected on a wall with about ten other people.

It was a Japanese movie about a "gross, broke" man who falls in love with a "beautiful, kind" woman. It wrapped up with the message that it's important to be yourself, and there was a scene partway through where both the man and the woman screamed their insecurities and rage at the sea.

"Yeah, there are some things you can only say to the sea."

After the movie, people who seemed to be regulars started sharing impressions. I got nervous wondering if I would have to say something, too, when another first-timer said, "I like movies, and in college I was a member of this film club . . ." and he said the name of that club.

That was Hakozaki, and I said, "What?! Me, too!"

"Huh?!"

For some reason I pulled my feet under me to sit more formally before telling him I had been in that club, the one that went bankrupt.

"Wow! What a miracle that we met randomly at a curry place," said Hakozaki.

"Ah-ha-ha!" My sister next to me laughed at Hakozaki's exaggerated reaction.

*So, what's your name? What year were you born? Where do you live?* Hakozaki asked question after question, and as the others discussed the movie, Hakozaki, me, and my amused sister made small talk.

He was two years older than me, working at an advertising company; I had graduated college but didn't get a full-time job and was just working part time. I didn't know what I wanted to do and didn't feel like becoming a company employee. I had lots of friends and classmates who didn't know what they wanted to do, and some friends of mine either couldn't job hunt or weren't sure if they should because right as they were starting their senior year, the Tohoku earthquake and tsunami had happened. Still, most job hunted and joined a company.

"Why do you think that is?" I had asked my sister, who is five years younger and was still a high schooler at the time.

"What choice did they have? You have to get a job and work—especially with the way the world is these days," she answered a bit angrily, and I thought, *Wow, she sounds so mature.*

"*Nnnngh!* It's a miracle!" Hakozaki said over and over. "It's a miracle we met here!"

I thought he was being melodramatic, but I laughed anyway. The day before our wedding, we were walking along the Kamo River and he confessed that the older founding club member who had gotten sick and used all the dues for surgery was him.

*What kind of lie is that?* I had laughed, and Hakozaki said, "Just kidding, just kidding," so I thought it must have been true. When I asked if he was all right now, he said, "Sure am!" The peppy reply sounded forced, which gave me a bad feeling, and I started to cry. Panicked, he took me to his house where he turned his closet inside out to find the medical records that showed his progress and latest physical results. It said that he didn't have a tumor anymore and

"You're healthy, but it seems like you're only eating fried foods?" so I cried out of relief.

After meeting at the curry joint, we ended up trading contact info and hanging out. Sometimes my sister joined us.

Since Hakozaki was a company employee, and I lived on part-time wages, our finances and lifestyles were different. Maybe he wanted to show me he had good taste? He kept picking slightly expensive restaurants to go to, so until we got to know each other well enough that I could say, "A cheaper place is fine, you know," I got more and more stressed each time we met.

I worked part time at a hotel in Kyoto. Back then, there weren't that many tourists, so I wasn't very busy. I killed time by refreshing social media and blocking anyone I found talking shit about someone.

Sometimes when I was working alone at night, my sister would come to visit. Really, it wasn't allowed, since she wasn't staying at the hotel, but I was bored, so I let her in through the back door and had her sit in the lobby on a sofa that didn't show on the security cameras. She had trouble sleeping at night. Apparently, at school she slept through all her classes.

"Do you ever just wanna be in the same space as someone you gel with?" she'd asked me. "Like you don't need to talk. You just want to be alone, but with someone—you ever have times like that?"

I nodded. I was happy to have her say to my face that I was someone she gelled with. She worked on her laptop while I did my job.

She wrote part time. She got paid to write (as well as sometimes translate) and promote and spread bogus product reviews, articles about quack medical treatments, and fake news about climate change, international conflicts, and whatnot.

"It's not as if I'm slandering anyone in particular," she said even though I hadn't said a word about her work. She did feel guilty in her own way.

The amount of money she could make was limited by the pace at which she could write, but there was no limit on the amount of guilt that could pile up. My sister was somewhat frail, so there weren't many jobs she could do; she had no choice but to consult with her body and choose based on that. When she was feeling physically unwell, her mood also slumped, so she could harass herself endlessly about the guilt.

"If it's killing you, why not get some different writing work?" I said.

"Even if I quit, someone else will do it, so it's better for me to write it—it's better for me to suffer; even if the articles are trash, I want to strive for honesty in style."

*If you write lies in an honest style, won't you just trick more people, making everything even more irredeemable . . . ?* That's what I thought, but I didn't say anything more. *That's her sense of justice, so if that's what she wants to do, she should do it.* I respected her in a half-hearted way.

I wish I had said something. But what?

When I told Hakozaki my sister had vanished, he took it pretty hard—to the point that he stayed home from work for a few days. Seeing him like that, I began to worry about him and felt my own pain recede. *Maybe I seek out people similar to myself . . .* I seemed to have discovered something, and it gave me a strange energy. But that didn't last very long, either. My sister was my little sister, but to Hakozaki she was just another person. Even if he was worried about her, he didn't suddenly burst into tears like me, and soon he was able to go to work. That was a good thing. I was glad he recovered.

At a cheap bar in Kiyamachi, Hakozaki asked, "Are you seeing anybody?"

Before I could answer, he said, "Oh, sorry." I had blatantly frowned.

I did want to meet someone, and I did think I would be happy to go out with someone, but I didn't like dating as a topic of conversation.

It was like a reaction to something massive. My not being on board with romance was merely a social phenomenon in the same way being on board with romance was, so I was lonely.

Everyone's human, and you never know when what you say or ask could be offensive. Conversations with broad subjects like "romance" or "men and women," are bound to alienate or hurt someone precisely because of how broad they are. For me, it was less about me being hurt by the conversation, but the fact that someone somewhere probably would be. The people I could imagine loomed even larger than me in my head and gave shape to me.

But I wanted to spend time being connected, so I talked about movies and TV shows I'd seen, novels I'd read. I didn't really talk about people, like I did with the water or my sister. Talking about media meant I didn't have to get into the other person's personal life. And they wouldn't get into mine, either. Hakozaki adapted to me. *He's nice*, I thought.

We didn't speak of romance again until that winter when he suddenly asked me out.

We went to a movie together, and afterward, on Hakozaki's suggestion, we went to see the lights the city put up each year. It was supposed to be a little ways west of the station, but nothing was twinkling at all. Hakozaki anxiously looked it up, and on the sponsoring company's website, it said that for financial reasons, they were canceling the lights that year.

"Are you serious?" Hakozaki said, squatting down by the bayberry trees that had been shining brightly the previous year and would be again the next. "You like things that sparkle, right? I really wanted to show you."

"No worries. Let's just walk," I said, and we strolled by the dawn redwoods lining the road a little farther down. The tons of cars passing by, probably because people expected a light display, were so noisy we could only talk in blips and blops. Saying things like, *It's so cold!* and *Sure is!* loud enough to hear over the cars was fun. Their headlights lit up Hakozaki and made his hair shine.

"I want you to be my girlfriend." He said it as we were returning to the bayberry trees after looping back past the dawn redwoods.

*Huh*, I thought. *So he likes me romantically.* Maybe he had been holding back because of me. He confessed his feelings without even knowing if I had a partner or someone I liked. Instead of posting pics to social media to seem coupley, having sex, and all the other things people do to make going-out-ness a fait accompli, he told me how he felt. At age twenty-six, a confession like that must have taken a lot of effort.

I didn't have romantic feelings for Hakozaki, but I was happy he liked me. I don't think I really understand what it means to have special feelings for someone; I always just liked whoever liked me. That's how it had been with all the people I'd dated. I wanted to return people's kindness.

"I'm glad," I said. "Thank you."

"Really? Wow!"

He was so happy he cried. For the six years until we got

married, he dated me even though he knew I wasn't really on board with romance. It's possible I made him feel lonely because our ideas about love didn't align.

When the three of us hung out and we told my sister, she said, "Wowzers!" and congratulated us. "So that's what's been going on." She grinned at us for a while and then said, "Oh, but what about our plan, then?"

"I'm still down," I said.

"Oh."

"Huh? Why?"

"Ah, I just wondered."

"If it's something you decided on before, you should do it," said Hakozaki.

My sister and I had been planning to move in together.

Her income had dropped, and I was happy to pay less rent.

The thing my sister had mentioned of sometimes wanting to be alone but with someone was something I felt, too. When things are rough, even if you can't explain why they are, it's reassuring to have a nonthreatening presence around. Back then—and maybe still—I was kind of addicted to social media; I had to look at all the tragedies in the trends and read everyone's reactions. It wasn't as if they had happened to me, but I was connected to major events from all over the world. My fingers and eyes would move before the thought of connecting even crossed my mind, and my heart hurt. I experienced things as if they had happened to me and felt ill. I was only reading social media, but that's how my imagination worked.

My sister and I lived in a traditional wooden town-house near Kitano Tenmangu. When we first saw the place, we both wanted it, but this was a rare opportunity to check out housing options, so we had the real estate agent show us around for the entire day. The last place we looked at was a condo on the fifteenth floor in the Kujo area near Kyoto Tower. The clouds flowing across the sky seemed to have been brushed through with a rake, and the western sun struck the city like a keyboard through the gaps, making it gleam. The real estate agent helping us chuckled vacantly and didn't seem very invested, so we enjoyed looking at the building without feeling guilty at all. We went onto the balcony and took a selfie with Kyoto Tower in the background. Once we were satisfied, we went back to the real estate office and did the contract for the townhouse.

I lived in that house with my sister for four years. We found out putting an air conditioner in would cost more than the real estate agent estimated. We figured, *Eh, we can make do with fans and heaters*, so the first summer and winter were tough. My sister started going to the curry shop screenings again, and things were going well with an art student she met there. Every time she got together with someone or broke up, I painted her favorite Pokémon on the wall.

"The more life experience you accrue, the more Squirtles you get, so keep at it!" I realized I wasn't exactly making sense, but it made my sister happy, anyhow.

Just as the season changed to fall, on a day the scent of osmanthus made it into the house, she was gone.

*Everything's fine,* said a letter left on the table.

There were clothes she had taken off and never washed strewn around her room, just like the day before; I called our parents, but she wasn't there. She had been missing for several days. *Maybe she just went on a trip somewhere with her phone off?* Despite that optimistic thought, I was worried.

Now two years had passed. I stayed living in that big place by myself. I wanted to stay and wait for my sister, even if I married Hakozaki. I didn't want to come to terms with the fact that she was gone. I didn't want to run from the fact that she wasn't coming back.

I sent a picture of Kohaku to her LINE account.

*Today Hakozaki and I went to a hedgehog café,* I wrote.

I also told her that he proposed. Maybe she would reply to something that packed such a punch. I watched the screen for a while, but I didn't even get a Read notification. *We met to discuss the ceremony. I got some weird water in the mail.* I had been messaging her every day since she disappeared, but she must not have been on LINE, or maybe she had gotten a new phone. Or maybe she couldn't see the messages for some other reason.

Maybe she would never see them. But I wrote because I wanted to believe she would.

The police couldn't find her, either.

They asked if I had any ideas why she might have left.

*She's writing fake news, and it's gradually, undoubtedly, creating opportunities for division by categorizing people as something—"Men" and "women," "Japanese people" and "foreigners"—but the consequences of her not doing it would be even worse . . . She's convinced of that, and it stresses her out . . .*

I wondered for a second if I should say those things.

My parents suggested I come home. They seemed to want me to. When I said, "I'm going to stay here and wait for Hinata," they sorrowfully said they understood and offered to pay my rent. I declined. I wanted to pay for it all myself. I wanted to be stubborn. I thought that would keep me connected to my sister.

I took more shifts at work and started to get tired, which made Hakozaki worry. The thought suddenly occurred to me in the bath one day: *Maybe we're getting married because I'm tired.*

I put my face in the water so my whole body would be submerged, and water got into my nose, which hurt, so I stayed like that for a little while. It seemed like the pain would banish my thoughts to somewhere else. I wanted to focus on how much it hurt forever.

We both had a day off and were waiting for the subway because Hakozaki suggested we go see some exhibition.

"About our living arrangements," he said. "I think we should be together."

"Huh? *Nnn*."

"Is that a yes *nnn* or a no *nnn*?"

"But you know, don't you?" I said. "I want to wait for my sister."

"Right."

"Huh?"

"Right. You're going to wait for Hinata forever, yeah?"

"Yeah. So . . . what?"

"But we don't know when she's coming back. We don't even know if she will. Staying in that house will only wear you down."

"He said this horrible, horrible thing to me," I'd tell the water.

"I know that. I'm well aware. Don't meddle with how other people want to live their lives."

"I will meddle," Hakozaki said.

"Huh?"

"I will meddle! We're getting married, so we're gonna be

family. Things aren't like they used to be. I'll take care not to hurt you, but I'm going to say the hard stuff."

It seemed like we were going to fight. Hakozaki and I almost never argued.

"I want to free you, Hatsuoka," he said. His voice was loud, but he faltered, so I knew he realized how arrogant he sounded.

Hakozaki seemed to want to regulate me via this thing called "marriage." He wanted to counter this hope-curse of waiting for someone who wasn't coming back.

*Don't think you can change me with something so simple as marriage.*

That's what I wanted to say, but in the current situation, Hakozaki's emotions were bigger and stronger. Before I even realized it, I was adjusting the volume of my voice so as not to trouble the people around us at the station.

I didn't know what to do, so when the train came, I took his hand and got on.

I knew he was acting out of kindness.

We left the issue unresolved. I went to give my seat to a pregnant woman standing in the next car. When Hakozaki came after me, I moved to the next car. When we arrived, I jogged toward the museum so he wouldn't catch up. We saw the exhibition separately. But I had the warm feeling that he was always nearby. I was worried he might not keep coming after me.

"Don't think you can change me with something so simple as marriage," I said to the water and felt better.

It was so hot being stuck under those lights. Wondering what the point of it was, I smiled my face off. I thought Hakozaki would cry, but he didn't; then when I teasingly said, "You can cry, you know," he started to, which was cute. The venue was a chapel-like building that had nothing to do with any religion, but you could see a shrine-like building from the window, and the priest-like guy read the program like he was leading an office meeting, but then he started clapping when we cut the cake; it was much more "student union" than I expected, which was funny. And I found out Kimiko is a right-wing extremist online.

"What are you writing?" asked Hakozaki. After the ceremony, we were staying at a somewhat pricey hotel.

"Didn't I tell you? I write to my sister every day."

"Huh."

"Wanna see?"

"Really? You don't mind?"

I handed him my iPhone. He looked at LINE, wincing and laughing in turn. As he slowly scrolled with his thumb, his eyes filled with tears. Suddenly he yelped. "Whoa! Wah! Look!" He showed me the screen.

There were Read notifications.

At that exact moment, my sister had read my messages. When I gasped and put a hand to my mouth, my fingers began to shake, and I cried. A picture arrived. In it, my sister was walking across some bleak land with a single well that seemed to be in a foreign country. It said "Congratulations" on it. Then she sent more photos of her smiling and walking toward the camera. Then nothing happened for a minute. I tried asking how she was doing. *I'm good. I have to catch a boat, so I'm going to lose Wi-Fi, but let's video chat soon. I've picked up lots of life experience, so paint lots of Squirtles for me.* "I wanted to be the one to see the Read notifications cooooome," I whined to Hakozaki, thinking it was more the kind of thing I should say to the water.

# PEOPLE WHO TALK TO STUFFED ANIMALS ARE NICE

Mugito hadn't been at school in a while. She lived right next to the university, so Nanamori thought of dropping by after second period, but he had just started dating Shiraki the day before, and he thought she might not appreciate his going to another girl's house even if Mugito was a mutual friend (they weren't at the point where he had been able to confirm that detail yet), so he just sent a message on LINE instead.

—Are you okay?

Nanamori was nineteen, and it was his first time having a girlfriend.

*I just want a girlfriend.* The feeling had started when he entered university as a vague, ever-present desire, but the previous day, it had been particularly strong.

Most of the people in his club and at his part-time job were quiet. He was in a social environment that you could call comparatively subdued. Even so, everyone was talking about love.

Apparently romance was something everyone participated in as a matter of course. It concerned Nanamori that he was the only one who hadn't.

He knew what it felt like to like someone as a friend. He didn't know what it felt like to like someone romantically. He couldn't see the difference between the two.

*I wish I could fall in love and have fun like everybody else*, thought Nanamori.

A girl had told him she liked him before. It happened in high school.

There was a period where a group of girls dragged him around, calling him "cute, like a girl." Nanamori was 156 cm tall and weighed 45 kg. These numbers had hardly budged since he was a first-year. The girls made him go shopping with them, had him try on clothes; the women's clothing fit him perfectly, and they squealed with delight at how well makeup suited him. Since he didn't appear very manly, he was enjoyed as a safe version of a boy. And Nanamori himself had felt comfortable. The girls thought he was adorable and complimented him. It was the boys who teased him for being girly while making fun of the girls at the same time. *But I'm also a boy. I'm not a girl.* He had been raised among the boys. In order to not be cast out of their group, all he could do was mirror them and laugh along like an idiot.

In high school, Nanamori adjusted to match each vibe,

always smiling politely like a doll. When the girls laughed about how their boyfriends were the worst because they only got in touch when they wanted sex, or how creepy it was when some guy they didn't know, after constantly showing up at their work, confessed that he liked them, Nanamori laughed, too. While cleaning up after class, one of the hot guys would smile at a cheerful girl and say, "Hurry it up, cow!" and the girl would laugh and go, "You talkin' to me?" Nanamori laughed, too.

When he thought about those times, a bitterness filled his chest to bursting.

Nowadays, he thought maybe he had laughed because he was scared—of the society-like thing packed into the school. And his complicity in it.

But at the time, it had been fun. Hanging with friends, snacking outside, riding the different waves of fads, piling into photo booths for pictures with the girls or taking selfies together, playing badminton at the community center after school with the boys. At night in the countryside, you could see the stars so well it was frightening. When he walked his dog, sometimes deer would peer at him from the gaps between trees, and the smell of the mountain dirt lingered forever in his nose. During the haze before sleep and in his dreams, the scenery and lifestyle of his high school days raced through his mind, sometimes making him writhe with nostalgia.

That there was so much bitterness mixed in with the fun

surprised him. Swept along, he had laughed at anyone that didn't count as "us."

At nineteen, Nanamori was able to regret it.

Even though the continuity of his life since then was unbroken, he wanted to distance himself from "that" self.

In Nanamori's second year of high school, Aokawa confessed that she liked him.

She was one of the girls who dragged him around. She was interested in a boy named Yanatsuka, who was also in their class, and since Yanatsuka and Nanamori hung out together, she often asked about him.

When she said, "What kind of girl does Yana like?" Nanamori didn't know, because though Yanatsuka had asked him that question, he had never asked Yanatsuka; so he LINE'd him on the spot, and when the reply came—"Cute ones"—he repeated it to her.

"Huh? I wonder if I count. Am I cute? I wonder if I'm cute."

"I think it's really cute that you're asking me that right now," said Nanamori.

*What music does Yana like? What books? What do you like, Nanamori? I'm reading this book my big sister borrowed from the library and left lying around—it's really interesting. You should read it. And then recommend it to Yana.*

"Ask Yana if he likes long hair or short hair better!" she said, and when Yanatsuka replied, "Long, I guess," Aokawa started to grow her hair out, and Nanamori thought it was adorable how, every time he saw her, she would say, "My hair's longer, see?" *When Aokawa is happy, I'm happy. Does that mean I like Aokawa?* he wondered, but after she asked him out, he realized he liked her as a friend.

Her hair had grown down to about her collarbones when she said, "While I was having you ask all these questions for me, I started liking you, Nanamori. I want you to be my boyfriend."

Aokawa stood there blushing, and Nanamori thought, *She's so cute.* But that was all he thought.

"Sorry," he said. "Thanks. I'm happy, but I . . ."

"You like someone else?"

"No, I just don't know what to think."

Aokawa covered her eyes with her hands. Nanamori was horrified. *She's crying. So love is . . . ?* He took out a handkerchief, and when he touched her cheeks and fingers, where the tears were running, he could feel her pulse through the cloth. *So love is this . . . serious . . .*

He wasn't able to ask what made it that way. He decided to put some distance between him and the girls—because he felt bad about Aokawa. Yana had started going out with a girl from a different school—they attended cram school together—and before Nanamori knew it, his other friends had fallen in love as well. *I'd like to try it, too*, he thought. But he couldn't. He didn't understand love, and he felt that starting something casual would betray Aokawa; that was how he spent the rest of high school and the first year and a half of university.

Now it was the fall of his second year.

The previous day, the club Nanamori participated in had one of its rare drinking parties. Or more like, people had gathered, and it ended up being a drinking party. It happened at the little gallery where he worked part time. Nanamori was getting a good chunk of money from his parents, and he had also gotten a scholarship, so he only worked when the gallery needed help sending or receiving art for exhibitions, or when they were shorthanded for reception duties or whatever. *I have it easy*, thought Nanamori. The owner and his wife even said that any of the part-timers could use the space on the second floor however they liked on the gallery's day off.

Nanamori thought the owner and his wife were good people, or rather, simple souls. Right after Nanamori started, another student who had been working there stole a ton of money and vanished. The couple laughed it off without even calling the police—"Well, he must have needed it for something." Their hollow laughter made him sad. Seeing them continue to be kind to the part-timers as usual hurt as if a little pebble had fallen into his heart. Nanamori realized that the expensive sweets the owners always gave out—which they claimed they received as gifts, so they were just sharing—were actually bought expressly for the workers, but he pretended not to notice for the couple's sake. He started visiting the second floor even when he didn't have anything particular to do, to show them that he was fond of the space—because it made them happy.

Since Mugito hadn't been at school, he had extra free time, so he had gone to the gallery.

He arrived to find his club president, Mitsusaki, there. She was sitting at a table on the second floor with another part-timer, Itoshita, who was seven years older than Nanamori, and the owner and his wife, drinking beer and chatting.

*Huh? The president and Itoshita?*

As far as Nanamori knew, the gallery and his club weren't connected. "Hey there," said the owner. Nanamori bobbed his head.

The others at the table were absorbed in their conversation. The owner's wife, Chikako, was saying, "I've never been to Kagoshima."

"Kagoshima?" Nanamori asked as he took a seat.

"Itoshita and Mitsu are going to go visit Itoshita's parents," said Chikako.

"Huh? Itoshita and Mitsusaki? What . . . ? Are you getting married . . . ?" Nanamori's reaction was rather loud—for Nanamori—and everyone laughed.

"No, we're not getting married," Mitsusaki said, looking delighted.

"We're not?" Itoshita joked.

"Not yet," flirted Mitsusaki.

Nanamori couldn't keep up.

"So you mean . . . huh? You two are going out?"

"Yeah! We didn't tell you?" Mitsusaki smiled. *I didn't know she had a smile like that*, thought Nanamori.

Mitsusaki was always sleeping in the clubroom, so Nanamori never had much chance to talk to her. Seeing his club president saying, "Lemme have some," as she happily shared drinks and snacks with her boyfriend made him feel awkward for some reason.

"No, you never told me. Wow. Where did you meet?" he asked, but she just glossed over it by saying, "Around." Apparently Mitsusaki came here often and was friends with the owner and Chikako.

The owner brought Nanamori a beer down from the couple's house on the third floor, and he drank it even though he didn't like alcohol. From the second-floor window, they could see the ginkgoes lining Horikawa-dori starting to turn color. When Nanamori said it was like they were at a cherry blossom–viewing party, Mitsusaki asked, "Should we call the other stuffed animal peeps? Would that be all right?" After checking with the owner and Chikako, Mitsusaki opened LINE.

—If you're at home and can come out, come on
  over.
—It's Nanamori, me, and the people from the
  gallery.
—We have booze!

She posted a drunk Rilakkuma sticker and the address
into the group LINE chat.

Nanamori figured it was too sudden of an invitation—
and so late in the day—for anyone to show up, but he was
hoping Mugito would come. Mugito was basically like a BFF
to him and had been since the beginning of his university
life. He had felt that for a while, but the feeling was even
stronger because he hadn't seen her in a long time.

In the end, it was Shiraki, Nishimura, and Fujio who
came, and the owner and Chikako seemed the most pleased
to see them.

*Ohh, so nice to meet you! What'll you have to drink? We have
plenty to choose from. Are you in the same year as Nanamori, Shiraki? Are you over twenty? Underage? If you are, don't go putting
this on social media.* They chuckled together.

Aside from Nanamori and Itoshita, the other young people were girls. *If the owner and Chikako had kids, I guess they
would be about our age,* thought Nanamori.

Apparently the three newcomers had no idea that their
president was going out with Itoshita, either; they all came

at different times, so they had to be filled in separately, which the president did with glee.

"Pics! Show us pics!" said Shiraki.

The president and Itoshita on vacation together with their faces poking through a cutout of a bipedal fish character facing sideways. A selfie against cherry blossoms. The president sleeping in the same posture as Itoshita's cat.

Shiraki leaned over Mitsusaki's phone and said, "Oh, you're so cute! Adorable!"

*Maybe I thought Aokawa was cute in the way that girls call each other cute.*

As the alcohol took effect, Nanamori wanted to say he was sorry. To Aokawa? For what, he wasn't sure.

Nanamori grew depressed, but cute was cute, and he was feeling toasty from drinking for the first time in a while. He opened the window, and as he was taking a look and enjoying the cool air, the evening sun was creeping over the ginkgoes, giving the leaves alternating tints of red and yellow through shifting patterns of light and shadow. *The way they sway in the breeze makes them look like butterflies*, he thought. *Can't the wind blow a little harder, so they come this way?* Thinking in that childlike way felt good, and as he was spacing out, everyone began talking about love.

The club was almost all girls. Even so, Nanamori almost never heard anyone talk about their love lives there. He figured maybe it was because the presence of the 350 stuffed animals loomed larger than humans. Maybe the reason they were talking about love now was that they were in a different environment. Or maybe it was because, at the moment, the strongest element in the atmosphere was the fact that Itoshita and the club president were a couple.

Shiraki had recently broken up with someone. Nanamori assumed it was the guy she had started dating before summer break, but as he listened, he learned that she had broken up with him during the break, and the guy she had broken up with the previous week had been new.

Nishimura had been in a relationship with another woman for nearly a year. Fujio had been invited on a group date and was talking with someone, though she wasn't sure if she would go out with them or not. The owner reminisced about the romances of his youth. Chikako's "What? You never told me that!" was like a punchline.

*Wow. Everyone is meeting people and making all sorts of romantic connections.*

It had been a long time since he had broken Aokawa's heart.

Really, he knew—that he didn't need to understand love. He knew that to simply get a lover, it was giving off the right vibes that was important, more so than really liking them.

*How about you, Nanamori?* someone asked.

"I'm not really . . ."

*This inability to connect, this feeling of being left out, going*

*out with someone or being incapable of going out with someone—
maybe I have a complex about it. I'll seem pathetic if I go through
college single.*

It made him wonder who of these people he might want
to date.

*Shiraki, I guess?*

They were the same age, in the same year, and didn't get
along badly, per se . . .

He had never gone somewhere with her on a day off like
with Mugito, but he could talk to her normally, and sometimes
they ate together. He heard she liked cats, so when he saw
one while he was out and about, he would take a picture and
send it to her. She sent him cat pictures, too. *We . . . get along
pretty well. It wouldn't be weird . . . if we dated . . .*

And Shiraki was dating and breaking up so often that
maybe it wouldn't be all that special if he asked her out. *And
if it's not special, maybe it'll be less stressful for the both of us.*

The sun set, and it grew late, so they called it a night.
The temperature was perfect; both his mind and body felt
light, no stiffness in his shoulders or fatigue. To Nanamori,
with his borderline delicate constitution, it was practically
euphoric. Maybe the alcohol was making him less fussy.
Chitchatting with Shiraki was tremendously fun. As they
walked, their hands brushed each other's. Imadegawa-dori
at one in the morning, with no cars or trains passing, no
other students . . .

When their conversation reached a pause, Nanamori ventured to ask her, "Hey, would you . . . wanna go out with me?"

"What . . . ? You like me, Nanamori?"

He wanted to say, *Y-yeah, I like you!*

But the "like" was a friend like.

So if he said he liked her, it would be a lie.

Shiraki could probably tell he didn't understand much about romance. But she still said, "Sure. I'm not seeing anyone right now."

*Gosh, she's so nice*, thought Nanamori.

She had given him the okay.

*Sweet!* he thought—less because he had succeeded in getting a girlfriend than because his asking didn't appear to have hurt her.

\* \* \*

Even if he didn't look threatening, he was a man. Nanamori realized that by asking a girl out, he became the opposite sex to her. If a man takes the romantic, lustful action of "confessing" his feelings to a woman, it could frighten or hurt her.

*I know that, but I still asked her out for my own selfish reasons.*

He felt guilty, but as he strode along in the pleasantly cool air, that lessened, and the happiness of her *sure* arrived after he got home. Shiraki's place was on Senbon-dori. After walking her there and saying, "I'm happy you said yes. See you tomorrow," Nanamori went back to his apartment in Shinmachi right next to the student union.

The building was currently being reinforced against earthquakes, and Nanamori was so giddy that, when he opened the window and saw the moonlight reflecting blindingly off the iron-pipe scaffolding that encased the reddish-brown exterior, he thought, *My heart!* He considered reporting the news to Mugito but decided against it.

The first thing Nanamori thought when he woke up the next morning was, again, how glad he was that he hadn't been a burden to Shiraki. Which is to say, maybe he was glad he hadn't gotten hurt.

After attending his first-period language class, he was free until fourth period, so he headed to the student union, which was seven minutes away from campus and one minute from his house.

The student union was full of clubrooms called "boxes," and the stuffed animal club (a.k.a. the "Plushie Club") Nanamori, Shiraki, and Mugito belonged to had gotten permission to use one the previous year.

In the single, eight-tatami-mat-size room, they had furniture, such as a couch and a bed, "donated" (more like thrown away) by clubmates living nearby and recent grads, as well as some still-usable electronics that had been abandoned at the student union junk drop, and there was a shower on the first floor of the building. Some club members lived there. Mitsusaki, the club president, was one of them, which made Nanamori think, *Oh, so she doesn't live with Itoshita.*

When Nanamori entered the room, Mitsusaki was sound asleep in the bed, and the vice president, Tarayama, was talking to a stuffed animal.

The public-facing agenda they used to get approved as a club stated that they collected and sewed their own stuffed animals. But their true purpose was to talk to them.

It was a gathering of university students who talked to stuffed animals. There were 110 members, but only around 15 of them actively came to the box. In order to avoid weirding out the freshmen who came to visit after seeing their fliers or informational pamphlets, no one talked to stuffed animals at the start of the school year in the spring. Once the newbies decided to join and had gotten used to the club, the upperclassman began talking to the stuffed animals, and any of the newbies who thought that was creepy stopped showing up. Of the fifteen members who stuck around, Shiraki and Nanamori were the only ones who didn't talk to stuffed animals. Nanamori simply never felt like he wanted to.

But he still liked the box. *People who talk to stuffed animals are nice. There are benefits to just having someone to talk to. That alone makes life a little easier.* Those were the words of the founder and vice president, who was on his fourth year as a senior after repeated leaves of absence and credit shortages.

*If you're having a hard time, it's better to talk to someone. But the person you direct those hardships at might get sad or hurt. That's why we should talk to stuffed animals. We can have the stuffed animals comfort us.*

Even though it was a stuffed animal club, Tarayama felt that if he as a guy were the president, girls would feel uncomfortable about joining, but conversely, him being there made it easier for guys to join, so he had been vice president for ages. He was poor, but he wasn't strong enough to make it as a working adult, so really, he wanted to live in the box, too. But he had a big, rugged body. *People would probably be freaked out if they came in the morning or at night to find me sleeping here . . .* Tarayama thought.

And the stuffed animals knew that. Because he told them.

The other club members he was close with didn't know in so many words, but they knew Tarayama to be kind and could sense that his life wasn't easy.

Tarayama had no intention of telling other people how hard things were for him—he was afraid it might hurt the feelings of those who would think, *Nah, no one would be scared of you,* or other people like him.

Tarayama was talking to a Winnie-the-Pooh plushie.

"What reason could there possibly be for people to kill each other? It's crazy. How could anyone do such a thing?

I ended up watching some news about a random shooting yesterday . . ."

Nanamori put on some noise-canceling headphones as he entered the room. They had a rule: No listening to what club members say to stuffed animals. But as Nanamori opened the door and the clubroom's light expanded before him, he caught the words "random shooting" and felt bad.

Nanamori knew that Tarayama never talked about that sort of thing outside the box.

At the beginning of September, he had gone to a café in Shijo-Kiyamachi after seeing a movie and heard Tarayama's voice from the second floor. Tarayama had been talking with people and laughing more than he ever had at the Plushie Club. Nanamori cracked up hearing him telling the others about going to karaoke with another group and even getting some laughs. *Is talking about karaoke really that much fun?* He was glad to know that Tarayama could laugh like that.

Some people were only able to get as depressed as they felt like inside the Plushie Club box. Tarayama was exactly that type, and that was the sort of atmosphere he cultivated for the club.

Nanamori didn't want to bother Tarayama and his friends, so he had stayed on the first floor and drunk a cup of chai, but before he finished it, the group came down to pay their bill. The two of them waved at each other awkwardly.

There had been three people in the group, and Nanamori didn't catch the face of the guy who paid for everyone. From behind, it had looked like Itoshita. The back of his hair was always cut too short. Once Nanamori thought it might be him, he couldn't see the person as anyone else.

Tarayama talked to Winnie-the-Pooh for ten minutes and then brushed him. This was something else mentioned in the club rules: Take good care of the stuffed animals.

When someone was brushing a stuffed animal, Nanamori made it a rule to not speak unless spoken to. He took special care not to disturb Tarayama, as his slow, careful brushing of the stuffed animals made it clear his attachment to them left no room for a third party.

Nanamori liked watching people brush the stuffed animals, and he liked watching people talk to them, too. He liked the sounds that weren't words he could hear through his noise-canceling headphones. They were fragmented, like scenery on the back of his closed eyelids that wouldn't come into focus, but he sensed instinctively that they were calming. Maybe he wanted to hear that.

*Next time I see Mugito, I'll tell her about this discovery. I should tell Shiraki, too.*

No one had ever asked Nanamori or Shiraki why they were in the club even though they didn't talk to stuffed animals. Most of the club members had trouble talking to people, and talking to stuffed animals was a private matter, so maybe they considered not talking to stuffed animals a private matter as well.

*I'll ask Shiraki why she joined even though she doesn't talk to stuffed animals*, thought Nanamori. Having made contact with another's kindness, he was feeling confident.

"Hey," Tarayama said bashfully after he finished brushing.

"Hi," said Nanamori.

"You had class first period?"

"German. I have it with Mugito, but she hasn't been coming. I'm free until fourth period."

"I see."

"Yeah."

Neither of them were very good conversationalists, and it was because they understood that that they talked in low voices, as if they were on intimate terms.

"What are you reading?"

"*Kaiji*."

"What part?"

"Where they're crossing the steel beams and then Sahara . . . with the air pressure. Tarayama, do you know Itoshita?"

"Yeah, we were in the same department. He graduated and did grad school somewhere else, but he's done with that, too. We also went to the same high school. We were in art club."

"Oh, huh."

As he listened, Nanamori thought, *I don't know much at all about Tarayama.* He didn't really know anything about the president, Nishimura, Fujio, or any of the other active Plushie Club members, either. Everyone was nice and avoided asking about or discussing personal topics. It was a kindness that was easily mistaken for superficiality or disinterest.

"Ah, you work at the gallery with him, right? When I ran into you at the café, he was there, too."

"Oh." Maybe Itoshita and Mitsusaki had met through him.

"Can I talk to a stuffed animal again?" Tarayama asked.

"Oh, sure. Of course, of course."

Nanamori put his headphones back on, and this time Tarayama sat not Pooh, but a rabbit next to him and began to talk.

*Tarayama is so cute talking to stuffed animals with his big beard*, thought Nanamori. *There are 350 stuffed animals in this room, and in the middle of that, there's us.* At some point, the president had started snoring.

While Tarayama was talking to the rabbit, Nanamori got a LINE message from Shiraki.

—Wanna go to Saizeriya?
—Oh, right. We're dating now . . . !
—C'mon, let's go!

She added a sticker.

Nanamori answered and raced out of the box, heading for the Saizeriya right near campus.

It was only just past eleven, but even so, the place was full of students and faculty avoiding the lunch rush. Shiraki ordered a lunch set, and Nanamori, who had a pretty big appetite considering his size and usually got a Hamburg steak and a Milanese doria, tried ordering the same thing as his girlfriend today.

Nanamori was in the literature department, and Shiraki was studying economics. They didn't have any classes in common, so they talked about the seminars that hadn't begun yet.

"The Japanese lit seminar doesn't seem to require an interview. At least, that's what Mugito was saying the other day. She usually orders a pancetta pizza. Have you seen her lately?"

"No . . ." said Shiraki. As Nanamori was realizing maybe he was talking too much about Mugito with her, she started messing with her iPhone, and Nanamori looked at his, too.

—Are you okay?

His LINE message to Mugito had been read.

*Maybe she needs time to respond.* He stared at the screen as Shiraki talked about social media.

Nanamori had Instagram, Twitter, and Facebook, but they

were all such a pain he didn't really update much. When he had free time, he would open the apps and check the trends, where he'd see sad news and the latest outrage; though he knew there was nothing necessarily wrong with that, it still made him feel awful.

Shiraki was talking about an advertisement that was causing a shitstorm on Twitter.

On social media, and especially Twitter, where people called for progress in women's rights, LGBTQ rights, and so on, blowups about gender were frequent. Incidents emblematic of contemporary society with its lack of gender equality—treatment between men and women, or women being expected to be feminine, or anything that furthered discrimination—were brought up and shared, and then tons of people would comment with criticism and demand change. But a lot of people didn't understand why others were yelling for an end of discrimination against women in particular. With ordinary things they had done suddenly being criticized, many felt like they and their ordinary lives were under attack.

It was only natural that incidents where people were being viewed only as some attribute, like sex or nationality, instead of as individuals, would elicit outrage, so even though seeing it made him feel awful, Nanamori felt that the outrage was a good thing.

Shiraki was looking at a picture of a huge poster that had

been hung in stations and buildings around Tokyo. It was an ad singing the praises of a society where women could play an active role, yet for some reason, it basically implied that working women had to turn male.

Nanamori looked at the same picture and thought, *I don't get it.* He felt like it was saying that women weren't suited for work, that in order to continue working, they had to mimic men and become part of male society, and that depressed him. It was almost like the ad was reinforcing the status quo to satisfy the closed-minded . . . *Yeah, of course that would blow up.* When he looked with a frown to Shiraki for agreement, he got a different reaction from what he was expecting.

"What's with these people? Seriously? It's just nonstop whining," she said. She wasn't annoyed with the ad, but with the people criticizing it. "Um, women take time off when they have kids. And the men work. So no wonder it's a male society and women have to be like men. Complaining won't change that."

*Why would she say that?* Nanamori wondered. He didn't know anyone who said things like that. *The reason she's speaking her mind to me must be because she's letting her guard down with her boyfriend? Because I'm the man who's her "boyfriend"?*

Nanamori had a hard time with comments about men and women being divided—he hated the topic. *Me and Shiraki are going out, but it's gross how just a man and a woman being together is enough to make people assume it's romantic and bug them about it. I wish they would look at people as people instead of as "men" and "women." I may be a man, but it's not as if my goal in life is for women to like me.*

Nanamori couldn't agree with Shiraki, but he didn't want to fight with his girlfriend, so he wanted to be done with this conversation. When he showed Shiraki a cat video that had appeared on his timeline, she smiled, which brought him happiness. His face smiled as if it was remembering the midnight giddiness. He felt warm and fuzzy. The depths of his heart were cold.

He liked Mugito better than Shiraki. He had been thinking it would be nice—no, wonderful—if he could date Mugito, but he also felt that no matter what relationship they were in, his current feelings toward her, that she was a great friend, wouldn't change, and actually, he was frightened that their friendship might vanish, and he didn't understand love, so he decided not to force romantic feelings for Mugito.

Yet he felt sad that he wasn't dating her.

*I don't even really understand the difference between friends and lovers, and now I have a girlfriend. This person isn't Mugito.* He knew having these thoughts was incredibly insulting to Shiraki.

Of the fifteen active Plushie Club members, everyone besides Tarayama and Nanamori were women. There was almost no talk of men and women or romance in the club box. While it was fun to talk about those things, it was also exhausting—because at times, you ended up conscious of turning people (and being turned) into something consumable.

Nanamori had found the atmosphere of middle and high school brutal, but he could relax in the Plushie Club. No one gossiped about who might be in love; the sexual energy in the room was muted. He was more comfortable here than he had been with the group of girls in high school. He was happy that he didn't have to be a boy or a girly boy or anything else. The more time he spent in the box, the fainter his sexual energy became, and the more the genderless part of him grew.

As a result, he sometimes subconsciously yearned to be categorized into sexually segregated groups, like things were before he entered university. When Nanamori heard the kids who occupied the back rows of the classroom talking as if college were an extension of middle and high school—"*That chick in the light music club was so damn cute.*" "*You totally could have bagged her!*"—the emotion that typically welled up inside him was hatred. *Look at people as people and not objects* . . . He thought the same thing over and over. And yet sometimes, his body ached with nostalgia for getting teased in his hometown about his appearance (which he was self-conscious about to begin with), his lacking masculinity, his complex about romance—for "that self," which had become something approaching an identity.

He had lived the longest not as his Plushie Club self, not as his self within the group of girls, but as his self in a place where men and women were separate.

So maybe the reason he asked Shiraki out wasn't just that they got along, but that an oppressive patriarchal gaze was implied in her femininity. He couldn't quite verbalize that himself yet, so her actions charmed him, and her words stung his throat.

After lunch, Shiraki headed to third period. Nanamori couldn't decide whether to go back to the box or hang out at home until fourth period. He was walking in the direction of both when he realized, *Oh, we didn't plan a date.* He LINE'd Shiraki.

—Wanna go to the zoo sometime?

He nearly sent "botanical garden" but thought better of it and decided on "zoo."

Then he thought of sending something to Mugito, and when he opened the app, a reply arrived from her.

—I'm okay.

When someone asked Mugito if she was okay, she only ever answered, *I'm okay.* Nanamori understood the feeling; he wished he hadn't asked anything.

\* \* \*

Mugito and Nanamori were both majoring in Japanese literature. They had met the previous spring at the department mixer.

The warm days continued, and the cherry blossom trees around campus bloomed bigger and sooner than other years, the uneasiness of the new students and their parents gathered on the flower petals, and the reach of the light expanded. It was sunny, and the temperature was just right. That alone made Nanamori feel healthy.

After the entrance ceremony, the students were split into departments and sent to an empty classroom in their faculty's building for a simple get-together. There were soft drinks and snacks, and the professors greeted and congratulated the new students, who stuck out in their suits. After an explanation of the credit and class system, the chair of the department said with a smile:

"Really, I'd like to have all 120 of you come up and introduce yourselves, but we can't do that due to time constraints, so please split into islands and get to know each other. Say your name, where you're from, your hobbies or special skills, your goals in this department, and hmm, what else? Your favorite book or author."

The new students winced at bit at the last item, which was clearly meant to get everyone excited.

"You don't say 'islands'?" the department chair asked. "Okay, groups, split into groups. Ah, whatever. Can the faculty members please guide the students?"

Nanamori had been in the back on the left, so he was rounded up by a young associate professor along with some other kids in the area.

Some people said they didn't like any author in particular. Some mulled: *My favorite book? Hmm . . .* Others ignored the prompts entirely. In a group of eighteen, Nanamori was the only one to name the book he did.

It was the book Aokawa had told him about.

*You should read it. And then recommend it to Yana*, she had said.

It was while he was reading that book that Aokawa confessed she had feelings for him. He felt he would regret setting it aside before finishing it, so he read the whole thing. It was good, so he wished he could simply think, *Hey, that was good*, but he didn't recommend it to Yana.

The reason he mentioned the book here was to diminish its association with breaking Aokawa's heart. To allow the book to exist on its own. To remind himself that he was in a different place now.

After about thirty minutes, everyone had finished their introductions. The head of the department stood up again.

"If you have time, please stay and chat, but anyone who needs to go home or run an errand can do so."

Nanamori was talking with a boy from his group while munching some cheese crackers and drinking lukewarm orange Fanta. The boy was still stuck on the topic of the Center Exam, but it wasn't required for this school, so Nanamori hadn't taken the test. Stretching the time out with the occasional murmur or nod was exhausting, so when the boy found a kid he had competed against in track and field in high school, Nanamori took the opportunity to drift away. Leaning against the back wall of the classroom, he watched all the people.

With 120 kids plus faculty and TAs in the medium-sized classroom, it was a pretty tight fit. Everyone was either finding someone they had things in common with or otherwise making friends by creating some. Chatty, considerate—as if advertising their role in the community they'd belonged to previously.

"Hey, did you just . . ." someone spoke to him.

She said the name of the book.

Nanamori had never heard anyone but Aokawa mention that book.

"Ah, yeah. That was me. It's a favorite of mine. Do you like it, too?"

Of the many ways he could have addressed her, he had chosen a casual form after hesitating for a moment, and immediately felt embarrassed.

"Yeah, it's a good one," she replied. "I've never met anyone else who said they like it."

"Oh, same. Um . . . what's your name?"

"Mugito. Mimiko Mugito. You write Mugito with the kanji for 'wheat' and 'door,' and Mimiko is 'beautiful sea child.' What's your name?"

Nanamori told her his name was Tsuyoshi Nanamori, and they both laughed at the jumble of formal and casual speech forms they were using.

People were starting to dribble out of the classroom. It wasn't even dinnertime yet, but some people probably had to go home, or back to their apartments where their parents were waiting; maybe they would go sightseeing in Kyoto.

"I'm so hungry. All we had to eat was potato chips," said Mugito.

"I had the cheese crackers. Do you live at home?"

"I'm in a rental. Near Demachiyanagi."

"I'm right near the . . . student union?"

"Oh, is it the building with the bright yellow carpeting in the hallways?"

"Huh? Yeah, that one."

"I went to look at it. The rent's cheap, so that's nice. That yellow carpeting is wild, though. I would have rather paid less rent, too, but Mother wouldn't let me move unless it was a place with autolocking doors."

"You call your mom 'Mother' . . . ?"

"I'm kidding."

"Oh. Are your parents here?"

"They left after the entrance ceremony."

"Mine, too. Wanna go get some food?"

"Sure, let's go."

The ceremonies for each department were at different times, which meant the restaurants near the university were busy all day. Nanamori and Mugito headed in a direction that seemed to be less crowded—"Is this north?" "Kyoto Tower is south, so this is north, yeah."—and climbed up the pedestrian bridge at Karasuma Teranouchi, where they checked the position of the tower, during which Nanamori thought, *I hope I'll keep seeing this girl.*

The two of them strolled north for fifteen minutes and went inside Kitaoji Vivre, but it was crowded with parents and kids from another school, so they tried heading east. When they crossed the bridge, they entered the botanical garden as if sucked in by the zelkovas lining the left side of the street.

Unfortunately, the greenhouse was already closed, but it was still a nice change of scenery. There was the pond and the rose garden, a square with a Victorianesque fountain, and best of all, cherry blossom trees in bloom.

Couples and families with children were having cherry blossom viewing parties in the open grassy area. Kids ran around screaming, *gyahhh!* It was Sunday—maybe there had been an event? There were adults wearing happi, and Mugito was delighted to spot a mascot character taking off their costume in the shade. The pair walked in a loop around the botanical garden. There was a forest area, and the trees that got damaged in the big typhoon hadn't been cleaned up.

"This seems like the kind of forest that would show up in a horror story or something," said Nanamori.

"I was just thinking the same thing!" Mugito said as she smiled at him.

After they wandered for a while, Mugito spoke up in a soft voice.

"He's really gone, huh."

"What?"

Mugito's throat seemed to catch at his response, as though she had realized he didn't know, as though it might be cruel to tell him. But she said the name.

The author of that book had died the previous year. But when Nanamori heard the news, the first thing he thought was, *But his characters are still alive.* Then he figured that if he thought that, maybe his heart wasn't actually hurting, so he decided not to say anything.

They walked through the forest, took a picture of the egret they found at the pond, and when they reached the fountain, Mugito was rubbing her eyes. She was crying.

"Are you okay?" Nanamori asked.

"I'm okay."

She was quietly weeping. *Should I rub her back?* Nanamori wondered. *But maybe that would scare her. We only just met.*

"I have a bunch of tissues, so . . ." he offered.

"Thanks."

"It's definitely a bummer when a favorite author dies . . ."

"It's not that. I just have allergies," Mugito said. "I took some medicine before the entrance ceremony, but my symptoms get worse when I'm hungry."

"Oh. Let's go get some food, then."

"Yeah. Something steaming hot. That'll be good for my eyes and nose."

*Maybe the truth is that she's sad* and *she has allergies,* thought Nanamori. *At least, that's what it would be if it were me,* he thought. *I can't believe I'm already relating to her so much . . .* The safe feeling of being with someone similar welled up inside him.

They left the botanical garden and walked and walked until they finally went into an udon shop near the university, though it was unclear whether it was actually open or not. "I write stories," said Mugito as she used her hands to hold her eyelids wide open over the steam. "I want to be a novelist. I haven't written anything lately, though."

It was the first time Nanamori had heard anyone mention such a thing without sounding sheepish.

"Huh. Wow."

"'Wow'?"

"Yeah. You have something you want to do, and you're actually doing it, right? That's great."

Nanamori didn't have any hobbies. There wasn't anything he wanted to do. With every question he asked, Mugito's
voice sparkled a little more, which made him happy. *She's
charming. I wish I wanted something that badly.*

"Maybe I should try my hand at something, too," ventured Nanamori, and Mugito shone even brighter.

The two of them met again the next day.

They planned to go over the course catalog and choose
classes together. Escaping the aisle of extracurricular club re-
cruitment, they went to the computer lab, and tried to find
two open seats next to each other. After registering for major
requirements, a foreign language, and some general educa-
tion courses, it turned out that Nanamori had about three
classes a day, a schedule that wasn't too heavy—but he did
have to go to his language class on Saturday.

The pair spent the better part of the day flipping through
the catalog and clicking at the computer.

They talked about whether to go strolling or check out
clubs, or what they should do. Nanamori, for his part, wanted
to walk around Kyoto with Mugito. The idea that she might
make better friends with someone else scared him. But he
disgusted himself with that thought, so when Mugito suggested they check out some clubs and then go out, he agreed
with exaggerated enthusiasm.

They sat down on a bench outside and, from the school
emblem bags they'd been given at the entrance ceremony,

pulled out the huge pile of club fliers they'd gotten from upperclassmen.

Recreational tennis, tea ceremony, the mineral research association, badminton, the actual tennis team, a swimming club, the historical ruins society, literature club, tanka poetry club, Greek club, a club for fans of baseball . . .

They had merely walked by, but with the new student bag marking them as freshmen, they had each received about forty fliers.

"I guess you're probably thinking lit club, Mugito?" Nanamori ventured.

"Hmm. I feel like thinking about novels on my own would be more efficient. What about you, Nanamori? Were you in any sports before?"

"I played volleyball in middle school, but the coach would get mad at the littlest things . . ."

"So not a sport."

Mugito weeded out the sports fliers and crumpled them up. *She's going to join the same club as me . . . !* The realization overwhelmed him.

"What about this?"

Mugito was holding a flier for the Plushie Club. It was printed monochromatically, which made the eyes of the Winnie-the-Pooh and Pikachu an unsettling pitch-black. Both of them were fans of things that were creepy-cute.

"Nice. I like the flier," he said.

"Should we go see what we can see?"

When they went to the box to see what they could see, Tarayama, the junior Nishimura, and sophomore Fujio were there. A handful of freshman girls interested in stuffed animals were visiting.

"How do you make stuffed animals?" Mugito asked, but since no one there knew—and it wasn't the right time to reveal that they talked to the stuffed animals—they evaded the question by chatting about things like: *What department are you in? Where are you from? Where are you living? The easiest gen-ed classes are . . . You should get your textbooks from an upperclassman.*

While they were in the box, Mugito touched some of the stuffed animals, took pictures, and began to get comfortable chatting with the other new girls. Nanamori had a hard time talking to people he was meeting for the first time, so he felt a bit anxious with only Mugito to rely on.

"Where'd you two meet? High school?" Nishimura asked.

"Oh, no, we're in the same department," said Nanamori.

Then, in a burst of bravado that said, *Of everyone here, I'm the one who gets along with her best,* he said, "Right, Mugito?" He made them sound like pals. Mugito cracked up at that, which made him extremely happy.

After about thirty minutes, they left, and Mugito said, "Let's come again. They're definitely up to something."

And so, three days later, they decided to visit in the middle of the night.

Since the main gate to the student union was closed, they had to use the side entrance by scanning their student IDs and inputting a password. Neither of them knew the password, so they waited until an upperclassman they didn't know went in, and snuck in behind them, giggling about how it was like they were trespassing.

The student union looked almost like an apartment building with lights on here and there. Every now and then they heard a chaotic cheer. *That's college kids for you!* thought Nanamori excitedly.

When they arrived on the floor with the Plushie Club, they heard a voice from beyond the closed door, and upon opening it, they found Tarayama talking to a stuffed animal.

"Why do they think they're better than everyone else? Just because other people exist doesn't make it a crisis. It's not even based in the real world, but they fabricate it themselves, make their opinions and emotions about this 'crisis' more real than reality, get all riled up . . . What's that about? It's so childish."

*What is he talking about?* Nanamori and Mugito exchanged a glance, and then—"Oh!"—Tarayama noticed them.

"Uh, err, you two came the other day, right? I was just, um—ha-ha . . ."

He hid the stuffed animal behind his back and looked to Mitsusaki, who was over on the bed, for advice about how to explain talking to stuffed animals. But Mitsusaki was asleep.

"No worries," said Mugito. "I don't think talking to stuffed animals is so strange. It's nice, isn't it? To talk and listen."

Mugito's eyes were open wide, and the way the reflection of hundreds of stuffed animals colored her pupils was really pretty.

That was why, later on, Nanamori asked her, "Want to join that club?"

Nanamori and Mugito always went around together. They had most of their classes together, and they always showed up at Plushie Club together. Once Nishimura told them, "You two are like twins. Always together, similar builds and haircuts." As they grew closer, Nanamori began to worry: *What'll I do if she gets a boyfriend and stops hanging out with me?*

Mugito talked to stuffed animals.

*She must just imagine them speaking the words in her head and then answer accordingly*, thought Nanamori.

He'd heard an interesting story from Nishimura. Apparently she had tried talking to a stuffed animal on the train.

"No one thought anything of it. I complained about people to the face of the stuffed animal poking out of my open bag, but I had earbuds in, so it looked like I was on the phone with someone."

She had put a stuffed animal in her bag to go to take pictures at a photo booth with her girlfriend. It had been her girlfriend's idea—*Let's take one last round for the Heisei era!* Her girlfriend knew about what kind of place the Plushie Club was, but she didn't know what Nishimura talked to the stuffed animals about.

When Nishimura came out as a lesbian to people at school or work, she felt like it put a limit on the way people could talk. The *I respect you!* atmosphere made her sick. That's what she complained to the stuffed animal about. "I feel like they stop seeing me as me," she had said on the train. "Plushie Club is better. Or more like, they don't care about people's sexualities or any of that stuff, so I can breathe easy there."

When she took purikura photos at an arcade with her girlfriend and a stuffed animal, she felt super valid, thriving. They'd been to take pictures many times since. It was like a cute drug.

"What's interesting," Nishimura said innocently, "is that there are so many people who make hands-free calls that if I hid my ears behind my hair, I'd be able to talk even without buds in because people would assume I was wearing them and figure I was on a call."

*The fact that it's impossible to tell the difference between people talking to themselves because they're struggling and people talking to someone on the phone is "interesting"?* Then, thought Nanamori, *couldn't it be that there's no good way to tell the difference between someone who pretends they're answering a stuffed animal, someone who's having a hard time and actually talking to themselves, and someone who really can hear stuffed animals' voices?*

*Mugito is just pretending, right?*

Somehow, the thought made Nanamori's heart beat faster, and though it was wrong, he secretly tried to listen in on Mugito's conversation with her stuffed animal. Pretending to itch his temple, he lifted the right noise-canceling headphone off of his ear slightly.

"Yeah, that's rough," Mugito was saying to the stuffed animal.

That had happened at the beginning of fall in their second year—the end of September—and since then, Mugito had stopped coming to school.

Now it was November.

When Nanamori went to the box after lunch with Shiraki, Mitsusaki was awake.

"One of the stuffed animals has been missing for a while. Do you know where it might have gone?"

Nanamori didn't know.

*Maybe*, he thought, *it has something to do with Mugito being gone.*

* * *

*Is it because I heard her?*

Nanamori occasionally wondered. He thought about how Mugito wasn't coming to school, hoping that it was only that. It would be so much easier if a cause or reason would pop into place. If it was his fault, all he would have to do was punish himself.

*Mugito, Mugito, are you okay?* he thought, on a date with Shiraki. The couple had met as planned a week later to go to the zoo.

Animals are cute. They got to hold hamsters. Nanamori became completely absorbed in the cuteness. The emotions that reflexively arose made the moment satisfying. *There is only this moment.* The anguish outside the cuteness disappeared. In his arms was a hamster, and next to him was Shiraki.

Nanamori's hamster was named Kurogoma, and Shiraki's was named Tokorozawa.

"Their names are too human!"

The pair laughed, echoing *So cute, so cute* back and forth.

"Wow!"

Moved by the black panthers, Nanamori got Shiraki and

the panthers in the frame and took a selfie in front of the cage. "Wow," he repeated.

"You're so girly, Nanamori," Shiraki said.

"Huh? Would you like it if I were more, uh . . . manly?"

"No, you don't have to force it. I was just thinking, 'That's so Nanamori.' I like that about you. Though it's not a boyfriend kind of like."

*Shiraki doesn't like me as a boyfriend, but she's going out with me. How can you go out with someone if you don't like them like that?*

*Why did I think I wanted to go out with Shiraki anyway? If it was just to go out with someone, then I've already done that.*

On their way home, among the museum, theater, temple, and other buildings lining the street, there stood a lone love hotel, colors faded like an old, beat-up toy. *It's not like we can't see it—walking past* without *laughing at how it doesn't seem to fit in on this street might actually seem more self-conscious.*

"Wow, it's really run down," Nanamori volunteered.

"Is it even open?" said Shiraki.

Nanamori fidgeted, wondering if people asked, *Wanna go in?* just as something to say, regardless of whether they felt like doing it or not.

"I wonder." Shiraki peered into Nanamori's face.

"What . . . ?"

"Nothing," she laughed.

Fallen leaves whirled on the wind. Orange sky. They huddled close against the updrafts caused by the subway. He walked Shiraki home.

"Wanna come in for tea?"

"Uh, okay."

The silence as the automatic lock to Shiraki's apartment building opened. The length of the silence as they rode the elevator to the eleventh floor. It was dim in the tiled hallway with no way to see outside. Their footsteps made no sounds, and Nanamori thought, *I'm glad she didn't wear heels today.* He had seen a number of couples where the woman was wearing heels despite being at the zoo. *I guess I'm not making her try too hard,* he thought. People seemed to be able to relax around him, a fact Nanamori was proud of. *I hope we can just have tea in her room without things getting tense.*

The studio apartment was sixteen or seventeen square meters, and Shiraki had pretty much the same IKEA furniture as Nanamori, but everything smelled entirely too good . . . He marveled at all the creams and sprays arrayed on her desk and shelves.

"Would you rather have tea or a drink?"

"Oh, I'm good with tea."

Nanamori didn't like alcohol. He hated getting drunk and he hated being around drunk people. Alcohol made people obnoxious, and it angered him that they used their intoxication as an excuse for misbehaving. But he did drink sometimes. *When I asked Shiraki out last week, I had already sobered up, right?*

In the new year, he would have his Coming of Age ceremony back in his hometown, and just the thought of the drinking party with his former classmates that would surely follow made him despair. During his time with the Plushie Club, that middle and high school energy he once found so uncomfortable had become distinctly loathsome. He knew the boys would tease him, *Tsuyoshi, do you have a girlfriend? Tsuyoshi, are you a virgin?*

Nanamori was happy that Shiraki prepared two cups of tea. It was evening, and sunlight was slanting through the room. The steam melted their shadows on the wall.

"Are you cold?" Shiraki whispered. The window had been open when they came inside. Nanamori shook his head and Shiraki laughed softly. A little while later, Nanamori got up to close the window, but instead, the evening light sucked him out onto the balcony. The temperature was perfect. Birds wheeled. To his left, written on the mountain, he could see the character for "big" that was set on fire for the Daimonji Yaki festival. As he stared at it, night fell.

"You wanna stay over?" Shiraki asked.

He was nervous.

"Sure."

He said it after waiting what seemed like an appropriate amount of time—not too long, since he felt that might be rude. He borrowed her shower. Then came the sound of Shiraki showering.

Nanamori had let his guard down awfully low—to both Shiraki and her room—but he couldn't handle this. He had reached his limit.

"Wanna come over here?" Shiraki asked.

"Sure."

He got into the bed. It smelled entirely too good. Their hands seemed about to hold each other. *Is this how you end up having sex?*

*I guess you just "end up" having it, huh?* was his sense.

It scared him.

Nanamori had a sex drive. But he always found himself thinking sex was like violence. He felt as though he was complicit in the conversations the boys in high school had—*Who's the cutest girl in our class? Who do you wanna do it with?* Porno mags, adult videos . . . When he imagined the sex he had never had, what came to mind was how women were only judged by their looks. He hated that. *Besides, I can take care of it myself . . . I'm hard . . . Don't get hard . . . I'm scared. With sexual desire, I just . . . there's no way. If I'm fine on my own, then I'd rather be fine on my own.* He let go of Shiraki's hand.

As he stared at the ceiling, he felt like he should say something, but he couldn't. If they were going to do it, he wished Shiraki would initiate. But Shiraki didn't do anything, either. She didn't say anything. *Is she waiting for me to make a move?*

More than a few minutes passed as he stared at the ceiling. He released a slow, audible breath and pretended to be asleep. He remained like that till morning, unable to doze off.

Without a word to Shiraki, he got out of bed at around five and went home.

—Sorry, I forgot I had work in the morning.
—I have to help carry in the new art super early.
—See you later.

In the train, Nanamori LINE'd Shiraki lies. She replied, *See you later*, right away, so he wondered if she had been awake.

When, after two weeks of him not contacting her at all, Shiraki said, "Let's break up," Nanamori was relieved.

He felt sad that he couldn't bring himself to say no.

*I won't even ask her why.*

When he said, "I guess we had a pretty good relationship, huh?" he felt awfully insensitive. *Maybe I'm drunk on myself*, he thought.

"I think so. You left a bit to be desired as a boyfriend, though," she said with a smile.

When Nanamori tried replying, "Yeah," with a smile, Shiraki smiled back again.

*I like you, Shiraki*, he thought. But he didn't say it—because he liked her not as a girlfriend, but as a person. *Once we're better friends and I can say it casually, then I'll tell her.* He felt like the immensity of romance had been somewhat diminished by breaking up with someone. He was glad he had been able to split with Shiraki before they had become what you could truly call "lovers."

There were lights wrapped around the fir tree outside the library. As Nanamori and Shiraki sat on a bench of something like gray marble, it grew dark, and the tree lights came on.

It was late November, the final day of the school festival. *Year after year, when it gets to be this season, maybe I'll recall how Shiraki and I broke up here. To make sure the way it looks from the outside—that the girl I asked out dumped me after only a month—doesn't find its way in, I need to fill every nook and cranny of my memory with the warmth of this moment*, thought Nanamori.

Shiraki had a blob of cotton on her lap; it floated, pale, like a flower in the night.

It was a stuffed animal she had made for the festival.

Plushie Club members were averse to the party atmosphere of the festival for the most part and generally stayed away from campus and the student union for the duration, but Tarayama had said, "Why don't we do something this year? Anyone who doesn't want to participate doesn't have to. I'm always just telling the stuffed animals about awful stuff, so I thought maybe they would be happy if I made them some friends."

So the club would open a stall selling original stuffed animals.

"You in, Nanamori?"

At the invitation, Nanamori asked Shiraki, "How about you, too?"

Ten members decided to make stuffed animals, but no one knew how. When they looked it up, it seemed complicated, so despite having been the one to come up with the idea, Tarayama decided Pooh and the rabbit he usually talked to might feel lonely if he made new stuffed animals, so all he did was sew pockets into their clothing.

Nanamori and Shiraki weren't buddies with any of the stuffed animals, so they decided to try making some, but they came out horrible.

Cotton Ball was Shiraki's friend. She hadn't had time to make the skin, so it was just a lump of stuffing that she had given black fabric eyes.

Ghost was black cotton with white fabric for a right eye and yellow glass for the left. That was Nanamori's friend.

Most of the other members' stuffed animals didn't come out any better, and the ones whose did were that much more attached to their creations, so they didn't want to put them up for sale. In the end, the booth was simply for displaying the stuffed animals and chatting—if they felt up to it—with anyone who stopped. That haphazardness felt on-brand for the Plushie Club, and the members were satisfied with it.

"Cotton Ball is cute," said Nanamori.

"Hm? Yeah, Ghost is cute, too," said Shiraki.

Ghost melted into the night, completely invisible. Occasionally, a light from the booths being broken down at the end of the day made its left eye shine.

"Hey, Shiraki."

"Yeah?"

"Are you ever going to talk to the stuffed animals?" Nanamori asked, and Shiraki smiled wryly.

"Nope. I'm not that type of person."

"'Type' . . . ? Then why are you in the Plushie Club?"

"Because when I say I'm in the Plushie Club, it goes over well with the guys in the meetup club I'm in."

"Oh . . . I see."

"But I'm glad I joined," Shiraki said. "There's a lot of borderline sexual harassment in the other club."

"Ah, really? Are you going to quit?"

"Nope. I feel more comfortable at Plushie Club, but places like that are pretty rare in this world, right?"

"'In this world' . . . ?"

"If I never leave those places, I won't be able to stand up for myself."

". . . Who cares if you can't stand up for yourself? There's nothing wrong with not being able to stand up for yourself. The problem is that people make you have to stand up in the first place."

*Is the world just one horrible incident after another . . . ?*

"But in reality, it's normal for horrible things to just happen."

It pained him that, in Shiraki's mind, horribleness was bound to happen as a law of nature.

Nanamori's voice went hoarse. "Is that why?"

"Why what?"

"I mean about a month ago when we went to eat at Saizeriya, you were saying all that stuff about women . . ."

"Was I?"

"Yeah. Maybe unconsciously? Were you saying those things without thinking? In that case, I really think you should quit your other club. In order to protect yourself from awful things, you're becoming awful yourself."

". . . Don't call me that."

"Sorry."

"That 'moral compass' of yours or whatever is exhausting. It feels like every other time I say something, you're scowling at me, Nanamori."

*Really?* Nanamori couldn't remember those times.

"After a while, I started thinking we might end up butting heads, and I didn't want to argue with you. You get so hurt by every little thing. And I wasn't sure if you really liked me or not, anyhow, so I said we should break up, and I thought we had a pretty smooth break, but then we ended up in this convo."

"You might not want to hear this, but I do actually like you, Shiraki. I realized after we broke up that I like you a ton as a friend."

*Why say that if you know she might not want to hear it?* he thought. His throat got tight, and his hands tensed. Ghost got squashed, and the part of the fluff that bulged out as a result made the glass eye touch Nanamori's finger.

"Plus, we have to talk. Without talking, you can't realize anything about the other person or yourself. Oh, maybe that's why everyone talks to stuffed animals—that could be it. They don't want to hurt people, but they have to talk, so they talk to the stuffed animals instead," he said.

"Uh . . . what are you talking about? Well, I guess Tarayama was saying the same kind of thing. Like even just having someone to listen helped . . ."

Shiraki smiled.

It was an awkward smile that came a few seconds after she spoke.

*Maybe she just wants to lighten the mood. Maybe she wants*

*to be done with this conversation.* Nanamori took the hint and played along.

"He's right!"

He tried chuckling—but it would be creepy if he laughed too much, so he adjusted his expression as he went. The wind was blowing hard, and the people breaking down the booths and the stage dropped a pipe; there was so much tension, it felt as though a slight ripple would be enough to make the whole atmosphere collapse.

*I need to head home before this moment gets ruined,* thought Nanamori.

"Well, see you later," he ventured.

"Yeah," Shiraki was kind enough to answer.

It was as if they had never decided to break up. It was like they were still dating or maybe like they never had been in the first place.

Since they were walking home in the same direction, Nanamori slowed down and waited for enough distance to come between them so they wouldn't have to talk anymore.

*Sorry.*

He was going to LINE her, but then he thought the only one who would feel better if he did was himself. Was sending a "Sorry" meant to coax an "I'm sorry, too" out of Shiraki? Would that make her feel better? The arrogance of the thought made him feel even worse. He knew he was thinking too hard, but for the moment, he wanted to wallow.

**\* \* \***

There was a two-week vacation after Christmas and then finals at the end of January. Mugito didn't have any attendance points, so it was possible she would fail her required classes. Given her circumstances, some professors might allow her to make up some with an extra report. No one—neither from the Plushie Club nor the department— knew what had happened to her. Nanamori crammed all the summaries and notes from the classes they shared into his bag and headed to her house.

It had been about three weeks since the breakup with Shiraki. Nanamori hadn't told anyone, but neither had he told anyone they were going out. Why not? Nanamori wasn't sure himself. Maybe it was because he had come this far with the guilt over just wanting a girlfriend still intact. What did everyone else do about the creepiness of wanting someone?

He walked through the Demachi Masugata shopping street, cutting through the December chill.

Nanamori hadn't spoken a word to Shiraki since the day they had broken up. He hadn't been to the gallery where he worked, either, because he felt like it would remind him of the day he asked her out. He hadn't been to the club box, and whenever he saw Shiraki around campus, he chose a different route.

He didn't have a single male friend he could drink and

laugh with at times like this. Sometimes he found himself thinking, *Maybe I'm a little scared of men—including my-self. And maybe as I continue to fear and dislike them, I end up making them into bigger villains than they actually are? For someone who thinks we should stop dividing people into "men" and "women," I'm doing an awful lot of dissing and discriminating.*

But just walking from his house, he overheard students chatting in the street:

"How many points?"

"Sixty-eight."

"Butt ugly, then."

"Nah, not so bad."

*I wish I could get angry. I wish I weren't scared of people capable of talking like that. If I weren't stuck with this body, if I were more solid and muscly, then . . . I might have called them out.*

*But wasn't I saying the same kind of stuff just a few years ago? Wasn't I laughing along?*

*I'm just as bad; everything would be so much easier if I could just get high on life in spite of that. I want . . . to call them out. I want to be able to get angry. But I'm scared. I just want people to realize that our actions could be hurting people. If only we could all just realize that and get along with each other and live healthy lives. I don't want anyone to feel as bad as I do now.*

*I wish I could suck up all that stuff—the aggressor nature, the stress of living—for everyone. If only I could just take on the burden of all the scary things, all the things that hurt people, and disappear,* came the thought like a sweet dream.

He crouched down. He was cold, and as he stared at his fingers, a hairline crack appeared in the skin. The words he was thinking—*I'm the worst*—were making him sick. His head hurt, and he threw up.

The color of the streetlight illuminated the dark shadows, blinking. A bird stood there motionless. Nanamori got a painkiller out of his bag and took it. It would be hard to see Mugito for the first time in so long feeling like this. He was practically in front of her house, but he turned back and did a loop of the arcade to calm himself down by spotting dogs and babies. He tried to picture his family's dog, but he couldn't.

Kyoto Animation had used this arcade as a location model, and a message of condolence was hanging up inside. When Nanamori was feeling bad, he absorbed other bad feelings. The helplessness he felt about the arson incident at the animation studio tied itself to his depressed feelings without him even realizing. The boundary between the miseries became indiscernible.

Pressing his temples as he walked, he entered the apartment building on the Kamo River. Standing in front of the autolocked door, he dialed the room number and pressed call.

"Mugito . . ." The hoarseness of his voice surprised him.

As he stood in front of the camera, his breath grew shallow in the poorly ventilated entryway.

In her room, Mugito was startled by the interphone noise and timidly checked the monitor.

*Oh, it's Nana . . .* she thought. The fish-eye lens showed him looking pale and tearful; it worried her so she let him in. If he had seemed fine, she probably would have had no qualms about ignoring him.

She couldn't just stand there; she went to the elevator to meet him without even bothering to change out of the loungewear T-shirt and shorts she had been wearing for days. When the elevator came up and the door opened, Mugito said, "Nana, are you okay?"

"Whoa—" Nanamori was surprised to find her waiting for him. "I'm . . . okay. You?"

"I'm okay, too."

Both of them worried about the other, trying to forget their own problems. *You don't seem okay . . .* they both thought. Mugito thought she would change and put on makeup once they got inside, act cheerful. *If my best friend feels so horrible, this is no time for me to feel horrible.*

"Oh right—first," said Nanamori as they walked to her room. "These are class notes and summaries I made copies of, heh-heh. You can have them, so come to finals."

He was so happy to see her that he laughed. He felt like a kid whose favorite person had come to pick them up at daycare, and when he entered her room, he felt even happier.

"I saw a dog a bit ago with a super pink butt! It was so cute. Oh, yeah—I made this! Its name is Ghost! I brought it because I wanted to show it to you. The Plushie Club had a booth. At the school festival. Tarayama said we should do something. Well, he didn't say it in Kansai dialect, but . . . I wonder why I said it in Kansai dialect. I have no idea. I don't know anything at all. Tarayama—you know, it seems like he's not doing too great. He was talking to a stuffed animal about a random shooting the other day. I wonder if he's okay. Maybe he's feeling bad. I wish we could just say we feel bad when we feel bad. For the festival, Tarayama made pockets for some of the stuffed animals. I made Ghost. Ahh, I should have made one for you, too. Let's make some together! We can make siblings!"

*Yikes*, thought Mugito. *Nana's out of control.* She felt like she was about to burst out laughing, which made it all the more painful to watch. *I wonder what happened. I wonder if it's okay to ask. He's shaking. He's scared. He can't tell anyone that he feels like this. I can't, either.*

"Are you cold?" asked Mugito. She turned the heat up, but he was still shaking.

Nanamori kept rambling excitedly; he couldn't ask why she hadn't been coming to school. As he pretended to be fine, his voice grew hoarse again. Different consonants from the words he was trying to say formed layers and came out of his throat. The more he talked, the more pitiful his voice sounded; it was a sound that seemed liable to outgrow its meanings and become more like an emotion, so he cleared his throat a number of times, trying to get rid of the rasp, but it wouldn't go away. It was like a curse.

Feeling like he was going to vomit, Nanamori said, "Tell me . . . why you weren't coming to school," as if praying for an answer.

Tears slid out of Mugito's eyes. *I'm crying.* When she looked into Nanamori's pupils and noticed her tears, they became waves. Nanamori's eyes filled with tears, too, and his wavered inside his eyelids for a little while without falling. Everything he saw through them became a blur. There, when Mugito felt like crying, she could.

*Nana's eyes blanket me, protecting me,* thought Mugito, and she leaned into that metaphor in order to create a sense of safety. *No one can see me clearly. Even to Nana, I look blurry. Right now I feel as calm as I do when I'm alone and self-harming.* Mugito sat on her bed and picked up a stuffed animal.

"I've been talking to this one," Mugito said, and she did smile.

*She's putting on a brave face.* Nanamori was disappointed in himself for making her bend over backward. *I wish we weren't human. It would be better if we were just one thing without mind, body, or words that fall out of sync. It would be so much better if language, society, and the individual were all equal realities, and the differences in our identities and our opinions were as simple as the words we say. Then anything that needs ending will end, and whatever needs to begin will begin.*

Without letting any of that resignation or anger show on his face or in his voice, Nanamori said: *Cute.*

"Cute. Can I touch it?"

"Sure." Mugito laughed as she handed it to him and said that she had brought it home from the box without permission.

It was an old-fashioned bear that had spent too much time in the sun—its light blue skin was faded; meanwhile, its white dress was so new it was jarring. The bear had no eyes. No nose. It did have a mouth and ears. Some of its fur had come out in places, exposing some of the white mesh beneath. There were burns and cuts, and since it had no eyes, those blemishes looked like eyes or other facial features.

The Plushie Club had never thrown out a stuffed animal, which meant they had lots of beat-up ones around. Some they found on the curb, others were left outside the box door by students who had heard of the club, and all were welcomed.

But there weren't any as injured as the one Mugito was holding. *Poor thing,* Nanamori thought, but then he wondered if it was really okay for someone else to decide what was poor, so he just called it cute again.

"Does it have a name . . . ?" he asked.

"No. I can't name it. I can't decide if giving it a name and making it someone new would be a relief or a curse. Maybe it would be fine to not think so hard and call it whatever came to mind. But it's a little too late for that. I've been talking to this one all fall."

Nanamori remembered overhearing Mugito talking to the stuffed animal—the time she had said, *Yeah, that's rough.*

"Hey, what have you been talking to the bear about?" said Nanamori. "You can tell me if you want. I want to share everything with you—even the rough stuff." He spoke as quietly as possible.

"Mm," said Mugito. She had the feeling Nanamori was someone she could talk to. "Umm, okay, but let me also tell you what happened leading up to me talking to it."

Nanamori nodded.

"At the end of summer vacation, I saw a pervert. A woman on a train was . . . getting pressed up against."

Just hearing that made a hole open up in Nanamori's chest.

"I was scared. It felt as if it were happening to me, and I couldn't do a thing."

*If I had been there*, thought Nanamori. *If it had been two of us, maybe we could have helped that person escape. Me being there might've comforted Mugito at least.* Thinking only made him more frustrated, until the thought, *Just die!* bubbled up in his mind. It wasn't Mugito's fault for not being able to stop the man. *The guy who did it should just die.* As Nanamori let his hatred out, he could tell it was scraping his heart.

"In middle school and high school, I heard from friends all the time," Mugito said, "stories about how they got groped. Those times I did think, *That sucks*, or *What a horrible guy*, but it was like striking a pose or something. It felt like an issue that didn't apply to me."

Nanamori hung his head. When Mugito saw that, she didn't know what to say. *My story is making Nana feel bad. But he told me to tell him, so I'll keep talking.*

"My friends would tell these stories all cheerful. Thinking back on it now, maybe it was like a barrier, though I'm not sure how aware of that they were. They couldn't break down in public. That sort of thing has never happened to me, not back then or now—well, maybe people have said things to me. Maybe I've been looked at in that way. Maybe just to live a 'normal' life as a girl, I've glossed over things to protect myself, too. I always thought sexual harassment, discrimination, assault, and all that stuff were unforgivable, but more as a matter of fact, not my own problem."

Mugito was scared to even talk about all this. There had never been anyone she could open up to about it. She had never thought she wanted to.

"After what I saw on the train, I wasn't myself anymore.

My old self disappeared. Since then, I've been more frightened of things like that. I'm sensitive to news about similar incidents—like, look how much it's happening! Look how much it's *been* happening! How did I even manage to live in this world until now? And living, being alive, it all just made me feel awful."

Mugito wiped at her tears—as if those things falling as she spoke were somehow not allowed.

"Life became unbearable. But luckily there was also a me with a bird's-eye view of the situation who knew that talking to someone might help; except, that might make them feel awful, so I thought I would talk to a stuffed animal, which is why I went to the box at the beginning of the fall semester. You heard me talking that time, right, Nana?"

"Yeah. I'm sorry."

"It's okay. I found this bear in the mountain of stuffed animals that day, and I had the same sparkly feeling I get when I find some clothes that look good on me. The space looked all bright, and the bear said, *I know how you feel. There's something I haven't been able to talk to anyone about, either, something hard that took who I always thought I was and changed me.* And I thought, *I know that feeling.* Maybe it doesn't make sense, but I felt like my story was this bear's and this bear's story was mine. *Yeah, that's rough,* I said to the bear as if it were totally natural. Someday I want to call this stuffed animal by its name." She wanted to say, *[Name], you're okay.*

"Is it saying something now?"

"Not now. It must be listening to our conversation. Hearing a stuffed animal talk made me wonder if I was mentally ill. When I went to a clinic, they told me that the fact I showed up to be checked out meant I'd managed to save myself, in a way, so I could come back in on a regular basis and see how it goes. But I never went back—because I'm okay. I am okay. I'm not the one having a rough time. This bear and the girl on the train. People who have things like that happen to them are the ones having a rough time. But when I listen to this bear talk, or when I watch the news, I feel sick. People scare me now."

Mugito tried to smile so Nanamori wouldn't feel too bad, but when she finished talking, the pain came on a delay, and the tears wouldn't stop.

Nanamori rubbed her back. But he didn't know what words he could offer. *I'm the same as you. I understand how you feel, Mugito.* That's what he wanted to say. But he couldn't. Because he wasn't the same. *I'm a man, and I'm privileged,* he ended up thinking.

After she calmed down, Mugito smiled and said, "That's why I couldn't meet up with anyone."

The two of them played *Smash Bros*. It was the Game-Cube version. Mugito had taken her big brother's copy from their parents' house without asking.

*That reminds me—was she going to do an extra year?*

"No, I think I can just pick up the credits I missed next year, I'll be fine."

"Oh, I see. Huh. So you can just pick up the credits."

"I'll try taking the finals, too. Thanks for the notes."

They both spoke without thinking too hard. They kept their eyes on the screen and manipulated their controllers at blistering speeds. They were fighting and did want to beat the other, but more than that, they were happy to be locked in this competitive battle dance. Each moment was burned into Nanamori's retinas faster than he could think the words, *It's so pretty*. For some reason, this happiness made him wish he had been born much further in the future. *In the far-flung future when society is embedded in a kindness where no one gets hurt.*

The two of them could stay wordless for any number of hours on end. A silence between comfortable companions wasn't a problem to begin with, but filtered through their enthusiasm, it began to gleam. Basking in that light, impressed or dejected in turn, they ended up playing *Smash* for five hours. For the last hour, Mugito must have noticed that Nanamori felt sad about leaving, and they both checked the time on their phones every few minutes, loath to say goodbye.

But Nanamori thought it would be better not to make this day anything special.

"I'm gonna head home."

As soon as he said it, he rushed out of her room.

When he entered the hallway, Mugito said, *See you,* and stood waving at the door forever, but he thought she would get cold waiting like that, so he opted not to wave back as he headed home.

The temperature outside was subzero. His body had been suffused with the warmth of the heater, so he was dizzy for a little while as the cold settled on top of him and the heat left. There was no one on the shopping street. It was the kind of silence that would improve a person's concentration, at least until they got too cold. Nanamori stuffed Ghost inside his scarf to warm up. He veered a little north to go to the grounds of Shokoku-ji Temple and tried talking to the stuffed animal.

"I felt pretty awful listening to Mugito's story. Really, I wanted to cry. I felt as bad as Mugito did, like her feelings were my own. Is that empathy, I guess? Is it important? I think it is. But I end up thinking that it's just me going out of my way to get hurt. Maybe I just want to be able to tell myself that I'm not aggressive. If I'm hurting, I couldn't be one of the bad ones. The thought that maybe I get hurt to make things easier on myself makes me feel even worse. But you know, I said I wanted us to share everything with each other, so who cares if I feel bad? I'm privileged. No one's ever violated me out of nowhere. It's my own words hurting myself. I'd rather just stop there. No matter how bad I feel, that's fine. I'm a man. I might frighten someone just by being there. As long as me feeling bad prevents other people from getting hurt, I'm happy."

*This is like a manifesto*, Nanamori thought. *Even if I forget, maybe Ghost will remember for me.*

* * *

Nanamori wanted to be like a tree or a rock or a ghost. He didn't care if he existed or not. He wasn't going to die, so he wanted to live a disappearing life. He abruptly tried bleaching his hair. *Maybe if my appearance is loud, my words and actions will leave less of an aftertaste.*

First he dyed it a light color, then he bleached it three times. His scalp got so irritated he developed scabs in a few places. Picking them off before bedtime was mildly pleasurable. For a while he had crazy dandruff. *But you can't see it because my hair is blond!*

He put some white bleach and maintenance shampoo into the suitcase he was packing to go home for New Year's. When his mother arrived to pick him up at the station, he suddenly got embarrassed and sat in the backseat of her car.

"Your hair!" she commented disapprovingly, before asking why.

"Why not?" said Nanamori. They drove over the countryside mountain, and he was sad to hear that the sole convenience store had just closed that day. There were cars in its parking lot and the shop's blinds were half closed; Nanamori could see several people from the waist down inside.

"Did you do it yourself?"

"Yeah."

"Wow. You really got all the color out."

His mother's curious eyes. She also seemed jealous. *This is going well*, he thought, of his blond hair. It became a topic of conversation when he was with people. He liked this sort of small talk. He hoped it would continue for a while, even with his family. It allowed him to keep his distance from people. It allowed him to keep people at a distance.

His mother spoke softly, and she was also hard of hearing. She must have been waiting for a red light to stop at because she turned around and said, looking straight at her son, "I dreamed about Gon yesterday. Because you were coming home."

The family dog had died while Nanamori was dating Shiraki, and he hadn't told her about it. The dog had been old, fifteen or sixteen. And he had been weak since Nanamori was in middle school, so he could have died any time.

—Gon died this morning.

His mom had told him via LINE.

—Oh.

That was his only reaction. He felt like Gon's death had already arrived back when he was in middle school, so he took the news calmly.

"When we get home, go give him a prayer," his mother said.

*So she wears glasses when she drives now . . .* Nanamori looked at his mother through the rearview mirror.

"Oh, I only need these at night," she said. "How about you? You spend all your time reading at school, right?"

"I don't need glasses yet."

His mother smiled with an *mm*. She was forty-something. His mother and father were both around fifty years old. Forty-what? He didn't know. He didn't know her birthday, either. *It's easier to notice the aging of my parents than the changes in myself. We're already that old.*

The thought of caring for his elderly parents in the future depressed him; Nanamori was an only child, and he didn't want to move back to the middle of nowhere. *What should I do?* For now, he could keep avoiding a concrete answer and remain at a loss.

When they got home, Nanamori went to the room with the family altar and pressed his palms together. The March he left for college, this room had basically been a closet. There had been all sorts of unused things standing along the wall, but they weren't there anymore. Gon was dead, so the room had been cleaned up. *I wonder how old he was?* He prayed to the picture of a younger Gon smiling toward the camera. *It's me*, thought Nanamori. *Thank you.*

He showed Gon Ghost. *I wouldn't mind if the vacuum cleaner was in here, or the old rice cooker, whatever*, he thought. Those things were familiar to Gon. Nanamori didn't know when he would be back next, so he showed Ghost to the blank wall where those sorts of items might stand again someday.

*The room will remember us as we are now and convey that to what's here in the future. I guess I'm sentimental.* He prayed to his grandparents. The smoke from the incense curled up toward the black-and-white photos of his ancestors.

*I wonder if I'll always remember Gon together with dating Shiraki.*

Gon was already a memory. That was how completely Nanamori had been living his life with the knowledge that Gon would die. But Shiraki wasn't a memory yet. After hearing about Mugito's troubles, he felt like he wanted to know more about the roughness of Shiraki's life, which didn't resemble the roughness of his or Mugito's. *Maybe we shouldn't have broken up. If I had said I didn't want to break up, even if our relationship went bad, we still would have had it—I could have become a source of calm for her.*

It had only been a month or two since the breakup. They would see each other at school. *Oh, we'll still run into each other, so it's not as if our relationship has ended. I should see her. We should meet up,* thought Nanamori.

*Oh,*

*is this,*

*no,*

*wait,*

*huh?*

*. . .*

*Am I*

*acting like a stalker . . . ?*

He shuddered.

*This mild fever in my heart. My feelings are one-sided; even if they aren't annoying to Shiraki, they're risky.*

*"We broke up," as words, are very clear. I should base my actions on that.*

"I had a girlfriend, but we broke up."

He told Gon to see how it felt. *I told Ghost, too,* he thought. *Maybe I'm telling the people in the photographs as well?* Shapes of things that had lived and shapes of living things got wedged between people, allowing Nanamori to be self-aware of words and relationships.

He pressed his palms together once more and endeavored to clear his mind for Gon and the others.

When he went into the living room, his mother was making dinner, and his father was watching television—he was calling out the answers to the quiz that the personalities on the screen couldn't get. *He must want Mom to hear him,* thought Nanamori. That scared him a bit. *It's like he's trying to assert his authority,* he found himself thinking.

"You dyed your hair?" his father asked him.

*He doesn't know the difference between dying and bleaching.* The conversation about Nanamori's hair, how school was going, his part-time job, and so on continued, and his father seemed a bit happy, though he didn't let it show on his face. Nanamori answered the questions matter-of-factly. This had always been the way of their father-son communication. He would have liked to be able to wave at each other, hug, and whatnot, but they were stuck with this crudeness.

*I wonder what it was like when I was little. Was he able to use cutesy language with me?*

Nanamori's mother did all the housework, scooped his father a second serving of rice, and brought him another can of beer once his first was empty. This scene of . . . typical Japanese countryside life irritated Nanamori, and he wondered if he should say something. *But is it really my place to reform their way of life? They only have the newspaper and TV—they don't use the internet, so would they be surprised?*

*It'd be nice if I had a premise,* he thought. *But what would that be? Would it be easier for them to change if my words were the premise? Maybe I'm thinking too hard. Maybe I could just make the simple comment that maybe Mom doesn't need to do everything.*

A world where the sexes were equal and lived together dividing labor based on their abilities . . . Imagining such a reasonable world felt like imagining something that *could have been, if only,* so it was hard to do. Unable to picture that lifestyle, Nanamori took on the better part of the housework his mother had always handled. *I hope hearing Mom thank me will have an effect on Dad.*

*I hope when I say, "You don't have to do everything, Mom," the sentiment rubs off on both of them, and no one's feelings get hurt.*

The day before Nanamori's Coming of Age ceremony, his father cooked dinner, did the dishes, and poured him and his mother's sake. Though Nanamori knew it was due to the special occasion of his coming of age, he was happy.

"Let's team up and give Mom something for her birthday," he said in the car on the way to the ceremony. His mother was doing her caretaking work. "I wonder what would be good," he said. "What does Mom like? What are her hobbies?"

*It sure took long enough, but maybe starting now as a family, we can give Mom some happiness.* Especially given how gloomy he felt about the impending ceremony, the thought made him extra hopeful.

His other classmates were arriving at the venue in carpools. But Nanamori's house was remote even for this rural area, so he had to deal with the embarrassment of having his dad drop him off. He had turned off notifications for both his middle and high school LINE group chats and hadn't sent any messages.

Anxiety hit him in the form of the January cold as he got out of the car—he felt isolated. Just wearing a suit made his body tense. Someone clapped his shoulder by the entrance.

"Tsuyopon!"

"Yana!"

Tsuyoshi Nanamori was known as "Tsuyopon" in this setting.

"Heyyyyy!"

"H-hey."

"It's been way too long!"

He wasn't sure if they had been "best friends," but they had palled around in middle and high school, and their teachers and friends would ask Yana if they wanted to know about Tsuyopon, and Tsuyopon if they wanted to know about Yana. Since starting university, however, they hadn't been in touch.

"And with bleached hair! A new look for college!"

Then Yana asked to confirm the name of his school; it was considered a school smart people went to, so Nanamori felt somewhat hesitant as he said that was the one.

"Are you in any clubs?"

"Uh . . ."

*If I tell him I'm in the Plushie Club, I'll have to explain a ton*, thought Nanamori. No one here knew him as he was in college. They all thought of him as Tsuyopon.

"I'm . . . in a movie-watching club."

"Huh. What the heck? That sounds fun. You're in Kyoto, right? I wish I could live on my own in Kyoto! Oh, hey, it's Ega!"

He went with Yana over to Ega. "You're blond!" Ega laughed.

Watching the girls in their kimonos hug and show off to each other, Yana and Ega—as if to say, *Hey, look over here! Come talk to us!*—started loudly imitating their language arts teacher like they used to do in high school. Nanamori couldn't laugh unless he forced a *ha-ha-ha*.

Together they had done karaoke, swapped manga, held Pokémon battles behind their electronic dictionary covers during class, gone to see movies, visited each other's houses, slept over, and spent tons of time on breaks at school and also walking to and from. "Like yesterday" was impossible, but he could remember those days with Yana and the guys like it had been a month or two ago. Even so, he was re-moved from them now.

When Yana asked about his life lately, he answered and asked the same question back, welcomed the answer, over and over. The conversation was such that the longer they talked, the more clearly he could grasp the space between them. *Yana might have changed, too.* Allowing for that possi-bility, Nanamori refrained from discussing anything deeper. There was something nice about seeing him after so long, so the gap he felt remained hidden until Yana found another friend and drifted away.

*I didn't realize I was this cold. I have no interest in Yana anymore. We don't click the way we used to, when having "inter-est" wasn't even something that would come to mind.* Time and space—it had only been two years of each. Overcoming that to have a relationship wouldn't even require traveling back in time, and yet . . .

The place he currently lived, his current life, his current friends wrapped his other friends up in the past. They created a distance, putting space between him and his past self.

The girls he had been close with in high school ap-proached him, waving. They all looked grown-up, and he thought they were pretty in their kimono. Aokawa was there, too. She awkwardly came to say hello.

"Nanamori, you seem more grown-up maybe?"

"Huh, you think so? It's not just because I'm wearing a

suit?" *I probably look even more like a child to her*, he thought. "You look really great in your kimono. So pretty."

"Thanks. You'll always be Nanamori, huh."

*Aokawa, I had a girlfriend.*

For the ceremony, they sat according to what middle school they had attended. Punks, like those who get covered on net news, heckled the presenter. They glared at the comedians sitting on the stage who had come to do a manzai performance. Yana was laughing at the guy who started mimicking the sign-language interpreter. Nanamori felt uncomfortable. *I used to be like him.*

His friend was showing him how much his environment had changed, and he felt lonely. *Maybe one day I'll feel estranged from Mugito, too. We just happen to be attending the same university. We'll graduate. We'll get jobs. If we move physically apart, everything else will naturally separate.*

If they were older and he had met Mugito or Yana in a place where he was more settled, he wouldn't have felt this lonely. He was happy he met them. He just wished he hadn't met them during this transitional period known as "studenthood." *Maybe I'm happy I met them because this loneliness is part of it. Is that . . . life . . . ?* The tears started coming, and they didn't stop; he was pointed out as one of the people moved by the speech given by their former classmate representative and the photo session, which everyone found amusing.

After the ceremony, there was some downtime, and then a middle school reunion that night. The vibe was that everyone would attend as a matter of course, so Nanamori couldn't beg out. Everyone drank like it was nothing.

Nanamori imagined the amount people would drink, like his father, for whom drinking was part of the work-life cycle, and the parents and older siblings of the other new adults present. It would fill this izakaya, and the ceremony venue, to bursting. *You can't get by in this world without drinking, huh . . . I really, truly hate this . . .* thought Nanamori as he sipped a beer.

"Tsuyopon, Tsuyopon!" Yana was waving him over from another table.

There were a lot of troublemakers over there; in middle school, they had been the popular group. Yana was tough enough to come and go between groups without really belonging to any, so the guys made him into their pet gofer.

When Nanamori decided to go over there, one of the guys complimented him, "Heyyy, Nanamori. It's been forever! The blond looks good." He was happy to get attention from someone that scary and loud. And that caused disgust with himself to mix into his emotions. *I hope they'll let me go soon*, he thought.

In middle school, they had asked him who he thought was the cutest in their class, and when he had innocently answered, "Asakura," they were all, "Ooh, Nanamori likes

Asakura!" and ribbed him for the next while. That scene was re-created at this party.

*I heard Asakura doesn't have a boyfriend at the moment. I have condoms if you want,* the guy sitting across from him was saying.

*Ahhh*—the guy was disappointed in Nanamori's lack of enthusiasm. He clicked his tongue in annoyance.

*Were they always making fun of me like this?* thought Nanamori. When he looked to his friend for backup, Yana was talking about how he took a girl home from a group blind date. When Yana was with the loud guys, he talked about things they would like, and used the nicknames that the group used. Here, Nanamori wasn't Tsuyopon. "Tsuyoshi, do you have a girlfriend?" Yana asked him. "Are you still a virgin?"

*If someone was going to ask me something so gross, why couldn't it have been one of the guys I don't like . . . ?*

*But I could have been one of them.*

"Does it matter?"

"Huh? You're not gay, are you?" Yana said, and the table cracked up.

"That *really* doesn't matter."

"Oh, so you are!"

They probably wanted him to laugh and deny it—*I am not!*—as if it were a joke. Because that would make things more fun.

Nanamori didn't say anything. He went to the bathroom without saying a word. He could hear people whispering behind him.

Someone did a double take when he walked in.

Nanamori was mistaken for a girl because of his short stature and blond hair.

Washing his hands, a man said, "Ew."

Nanamori threw up. He couldn't look at the man. He was scared to go back to his table. He was scared of that man, the troublemakers, and Yana all in the same way. *We all grew up in the same place. I know it's not their fault; it's the environment that created them that's the problem. But, but . . .* Nanamori stood in the hallway listening to the racket.

*Just let the racket go on and on. Don't go back to words. Don't have meaning. Just stay obnoxious noise. If only their— our—words could remain completely private.* If he could have closed his ears to the people saying awful things, and closed their mouths, and that could have been the end of it, perhaps he could have faced his fear. But that wasn't how it worked. *All words come with society attached. All words come from society.* It made Nanamori feel helpless, and he crouched down.

He started to feel sick. This same thing had happened on the way to Mugito's house. *I just happened to manage to slip out of one sphere, but the same thing will just keep happening between different spheres.*

*But I . . .* Nanamori intoned. *I shouldn't hate those guys.*
His consciousness was spread throughout his unwell body,
and he couldn't quite speak. He wanted to think that the
pain he was going through was holding hatred at bay.

*Are you okay?*

It was a member of the staff asking.

Nanamori answered that he was fine.

When he went back to the table and drank some water,
he felt like he was going to throw up, and he raced back to
the bathroom with a hand over his mouth. Yana called him
a cab, so he was able to go home.

—Sorry.

Yana's message came late that night, and Nanamori didn't
know how to respond. *What should I do? What should I have
done?* Nanamori couldn't escape wondering. He couldn't
even get angry—because he was afraid.

\* \* \*

Nanamori started having a hard time going anywhere there
were lots of people. His body had grown frightened of them.
After returning to Kyoto, he could only go to the nearest
convenience store. Constantly scrolling on social media,

whenever he came across a tragic event or insulting comments, his heart was so crushed he felt like it was happening to him. *No aggression, no harm, is separate from me.*

*I hope I can get mad someday,* he thought. *I want to be able to call out absurdities as absurd, to say things are hard when they're hard.* For now, he couldn't even do that, so first, he needed to do something about himself—about this feeling he had that he needed to do something.

Winter break ended, but Nanamori didn't return to school. Mugito got in touch a few times. He hated causing people to worry. He didn't want to contact anyone because he didn't want to be a burden.

He messaged her:

—A lot has been going on and I can't go to school right now.
—I might not be able to chat.

Mugito, for her part, was lonely. She sensed that he was being considerate by glossing over his issues with "a lot." She wished he would abandon that distance and tell her everything. A few days after receiving Nanamori's messages, she headed to the box. It was after they had gotten their exams back. Sometimes she heard the stuffed animal's voice, and sometimes she didn't. She was a bit nervous because she hadn't seen the Plushie Club members in a while, so when she opened the door, she led with a cheerful, "Hello!"

"Whoa! Been a while!" said Fujio, and their president, Mitsusaki, who had been sleeping, woke up and waved.

No one asked her where she had been. Because they were nice. It was very similar to indifference.

Shiraki was there, too, and this atmosphere of the club, where no one asked Mugito anything, made her wonder if this kindness wasn't mutually destructive. It was a space where you were validated just for being present, and your misery was also valid. But it felt to her like they were saying it was fine to not escape that funk. *Kindness is sad*, Shiraki thought. *It's dangerous. Kindness is scary.*

*Even if she ends up having painful memories, it might make her feel better . . .* Shiraki made up her mind to ask Mugito what had happened. Just then, Mugito spoke up.

"Nana and the stuffed animal listened to what I had to say, so I'm feeling a bit better."

Her tone implied that she didn't want people to worry and she didn't want to discuss the details. So Shiraki decided to ask something else.

"Was the stuffed animal Ghost?"

"No, not Ghost. My stuffed animal." Even as she said it, Mugito thought, *My stuffed animal?*

*I hate the way that makes it sound like a possession. I want* to know its name . . . *If I could call it by name, I wouldn't have to use words like "my."*

"Oh, that reminds me—this is for you," said Shiraki.

There was a fluffy white stuffed animal in Shiraki's hands; Mugito stared at it.

"Did you make it, Yui?" she asked, calling Shiraki by her first name.

"Yeah. For the festival."

*It looks a lot like Ghost,* thought Mugito.

As if Shiraki read her mind, she said, "It looks a lot like Ghost, right? I made it with Nanamori."

"Oh."

Mugito felt surprised, happy, and then a little . . . *I don't know. Is this how a parent feels? Or what a big sister feels for a little brother?* Giving herself over to a great happiness, she smiled.

Shiraki was surprised, too—because Mugito's smile wasn't the kind you'd see in the usual game of interactions; there was no hint of jealousy or suspicion. *Does Mugito know about us? I felt so lost when Nanamori asked me out. I was sad because it seemed like it didn't need to be me. But I was happy, too.*

*I want to be like Mugito; I want to be like Nanamori,* thought Shiraki. They were like a pair of kids whose genders were hard to guess. *They'll probably always remain themselves. We're going to get older. Our surroundings will change. We won't always have a place like the Plushie Club.*

*Mugito and Nanamori are nice, so they're bound to get hurt more than most people.* Upset, Shiraki looked down.

"Mugito, do you want to keep it?" Shiraki said and immediately regretted it.

"Huh? Please don't talk about stuffed animals like they're objects."

Shiraki felt relieved to be called out.

Mugito mentally chastised herself, *That's what I tell myself;* she had no idea that Shiraki was offering because she wanted to strengthen the solace-like magic Mugito and Nanamori found with each other.

Next to Mugito was Tarayama. He didn't say a word but smiled in a way that made it seem like he was trying too hard. Mugito recalled how Nanamori said he had been talking to a stuffed animal about a random shooting.

There had been another shooting that day—multiple, actually, and the incidents had trended on social media for hours. One of them the shooter had livestreamed. The video was taken in first person from a camera attached to the criminal's body, so it was like looking at a videogame screen. People were killed like it was nothing. Before going on his spree, the shooter had released a statement in which he wrote that white men like him were being discriminated against. He said that, with the expansion of rights for women, minorities, immigrants, and so on, men like him were losing rights that naturally belonged to them, so the only way to protect himself was to cull the others.

Mugito had avoided the video because she knew it would destroy her. *Tarayama must have watched it*, she thought. She wanted to reach out to him, but she didn't know what to say.

*I wonder if Nana watched it*, thought Mugito.

She hadn't been in touch with him since replying to his last message with, *Take it easy.* She wanted to wait for him. She felt like there was a kind of trust in her not saying anything.

In the next room, there was a loud burst. *Definitely a balloon*, thought Mugito. She was able to think that. In a different place, she might have mistaken it for a different sound. Mugito imagined herself hearing a popping balloon as a gunshot. *Is there time to wait?* Mugito took out her iPhone.

—Are you okay?

She LINE'd Nanamori. It turned Read right away. But the reply didn't come until five hours later.

—I'm okay.

That was all he said. Mugito got worried. *If it took him hours to make even this short reply, then maybe he's not that okay.*

As she headed for his place, she sent:

—Are you at home?
—I'll be there soon!

The messages turned Read right away again, but there was no reply.

Nanamori wasn't sure how to reply. He was indeed home. If he did nothing, Mugito would arrive. He didn't not want to see her. But . . .

He decided to wash his face and clean up his room a little. *What should I tell her?* Mugito was worried about him, so he wondered what he could say to put her at ease.

He heard someone running down the hall. Thinking it might be Mugito, he opened the door. And there she was, dripping with sweat.

"Whoa!" she said. "You're blond!"

"Oh, yeah," said Nanamori. "I haven't seen you since I bleached it." His blond was more like custard pudding with caramel sauce roots at this point, and his facial hair had grown a bit.

"How have you been lately?" Mugito asked once inside. "I was worried about you."

"There's just been a lot going on," said Nanamori; he didn't intend to tell her anything more. If he told her about what had happened to him, it could bring her down. *If I say "a lot," she'll get it,* he was thinking when he saw her eyes fill with tears.

"No," he said. "I'm sorry," he said.

"Huh?" said Mugito.

"I didn't want to make you sad. I thought if I told you about what upset me, the truth, that you would get hurt, too. So I . . ."

Nanamori's throat hurt. *Mugito's kindness and what I was trying to do by putting some distance between us are different things. Was my attempt at being considerate kindness?* Nanamori was scared, but he decided to talk about himself.

Slowly, choosing his words, Nanamori told her about what had happened at the Coming of Age ceremony and the reunion, taking care not to paint Yana and the others as villains. He told her about his mother and father. He told her how bad he had felt on his way to her house the previous winter. He told her about how uneasy he felt being a man, and how guilty.

"I might frighten people just by existing as a man. I hate being on the side of the aggressor . . ."

"But you haven't done anything, Nana. You're not frightening."

"That's because we're friends."

"Even if that's how you feel, I'm still going to say it. You didn't do anything wrong, Nana. I'm telling you you're not a bad guy—I don't even see you as a man. That day when you brought me the summaries and notes, I only talked about myself. I didn't make an effort to hear anything from you. So I'm really happy that you're telling me all this. Before I got here I was thinking you might not tell me anything. I thought I would have to get mad and say, 'Let me worry about you!' So thank you for allowing me to be concerned."

*You're not a bad guy—I don't even see you as a man.*

Hearing that made his heart fall to pieces. *Actually, I don't think of Mugito as a woman, either.*

Nanamori gave himself over to her with the words, "It's been rough. It's still so rough . . ."

He had thought in his head over and over how hard things were, but he hadn't told anyone until now. Imagining telling someone scared him so much he felt like he would collapse.

*But I said it.*

There was Mugito before him.

He was glad he had been able to tell her. His vulnerability as well as his affection for Mugito overflowed, and he spoke faster.

"When I'm with you . . . I—how do I put this—I feel like I'm a wonderful version of me. Things are 200 or 300 percent more wonderful when we're together."

He wanted to throw his arms around her.

"I love you, Mugito. It doesn't even have to be romantic; I just want to be with you even if one or the other of us dates someone or gets married. I want to be like a partner . . . to you."

"Same." *Same*, she said again, and then, "I love you, too, Nana."

It was such a relief to Nanamori that all he could do for the next little while was cry.

Mugito cried and smiled at the same time. "It's so hard," she said. She was still scared to get on the train. She could hear the stuffed animal's voice. She wasn't okay. But since neither of them were okay together, they were able to feel okay even though they weren't.

After they had calmed down, Nanamori told Mugito he had dated Shiraki.

"What!" said Mugito. "Not me?"

"Mm, yeah . . . Right, exactly. Maybe I was making Shiraki think, 'Not Mugito?' the whole time, from the very beginning. Back then, I was only thinking that I wanted a girlfriend, and I think she realized that and wasn't sure what to do."

"Hmm. Can I ask why you broke up?"

"I guess because we realized we weren't a romantic match. I think that's what she was telling me."

"So are you still friends?"

"I think so. Though we had a bit of a fight at the end. And since we're exes, it might be awkward to see each other at the box or wherever. Maybe it's better not to see her."

"Aren't you overthinking it? I mean, I don't know, but I think whatever will be will be. If you're friends. If neither of you hates the other, then it doesn't really matter, does it?"

"Maybe not."

"Yeah."

"I'm not sure, but I think I get it."

*If I see Shiraki once in a while, maybe that's fine*, thought Nanamori. He had asked someone out for the first time, gotten a girlfriend for the first time, broken up for the first time, and maybe without him realizing it, those firsts became a memorable event, something he was emotional about. *I won't worry about it so much. If I worry about it, it'll be all too easy to find myself back there again.*

* * *

It was spring. Six of the people from the Plushie Club box graduated. Tarayama was apparently still going to school, and Nanamori, Mugito, and Shiraki became juniors.

Nanamori had someone he could tell when he was

feeling bad. And he was thrilled it was Mugito. When she wasn't around, he talked to Ghost at home. He was still nervous about crowds because he felt there might be someone around who would say something scary, but he started attending lectures. He debated going to the box, and when he went, Shiraki was there.

"Long time no see," he said.

"Yeah. Nice hair," she replied.

"Thanks. How's it going?"

"It's going. You?"

"Same here. How about Cotton Ball?"

"Cotton Ball's at home. How about Ghost?"

Their conversation was like rain that wouldn't quite fall.

But as they met more often, the tempo picked up. Talking to Shiraki reminded Nanamori of their falling out, and his throat felt like it would close up. He couldn't deny the strategy of conforming for peace of mind. He thought, *Maybe by talking with Mugito and me, she'll change.* Though it seemed awfully arrogant to think so.

Younger students were listening to them talk. Could it be just as exhausting to hear people rail against social conventions as it was to hear people going along with them?

"Oh, yeah—I quit the other club. So I'll be here a lot more often."

"Really? I'm glad. But why'd you quit?"

"It's a secret." Shiraki smiled.

Someone knocked on the door, and when Nanamori opened it, a boy was standing there. It was someone new.

"Are you a freshman?" asked Nanamori.

"Yes, umm . . ."

"You came to check out the club?"

"Yes."

"Do you like stuffed animals?"

"Umm, I . . ."

His answers ended there. *Maybe he's not comfortable talking to people*, Nanamori thought, and he waited for a long time.

Suddenly the boy looked down and crouched into a ball.

"Does your stomach hurt? Are you okay?" asked Nanamori. "Do you want to lie down? Do you want to see a doctor?"

He could ask all the questions, but unless the boy answered, there was nothing he could do. "I'm okay," the boy said after a little while. "I'm okay, so it's okay."

*Something's bothering him*, thought Nanamori. He compared himself to the boy. He knew that an "okay" at a time like this didn't mean "okay," so he said, "If something's upsetting you, I'll listen. You can tell me. And I'll talk to you, too. If it's too hard to talk to a person right now, you can talk to a stuffed animal. Everyone here is friendly."

*You're too nice*, thought Shiraki. Seeing how Nanamori and Mugito got hurt, she wanted to free them from their niceness—Shiraki didn't talk to stuffed animals.

# BATH
# TOWEL
# VISUALS

A big bath towel. It was at my parents' house. Putting it over my head calmed me down. Among the smells, my parents, my little brother, and dog became images and clung to me. My brother would laugh, so I would turn into a ghost with the towel and try to walk around; all it takes to replay those moments is a deep breath in through my nose—even though now that I'm grown up, I don't have that towel anymore. I put a similarly big business hotel bath towel over my head and went to make things awkward.

"What are you doing?" asked Natsumoto.

"I'm a ghost," I said, wondering what my voice sounded like muffled.

"*Hya-hoo!*" laughed Natsumoto. I think we're dating. I never checked, but that's probably the right word for it.

"What's so funny?!" I wasn't sure if my irritation was getting through, so I spoke in a rough tone. It was hard to know when to take the towel off. I was glad it was time to check out.

I felt more untethered once I wasn't a ghost anymore. I

couldn't tell how loud the noises of the person next to me
and the cars going by were, and as we walked, Natsumoto
kicked the ground, his leg sweeping like a swing, and leaves
fluttered down. They fell haphazardly on the empty street,
and it was the next day, when I was clapping, that I thought,
*They were like applause.*

Dark silhouettes lined up behind the thin curtain. The
swirling colors and drumroll ended, and the spotlight
landed on the comedy duo that took first place. It was a pair
that made it to the finals of last year's M-1 Grand Prix.

We were supposed to list three acts we liked, and I put
their name down. They were popular, so it was a guaranteed
laugh. There were other people from TV, too, and even just
knowing that they had been on TV made me happy.

I didn't write the name of the duo my brother is part of.
Even though it had been my brother who told me to buy a
ticket, even though it was him I'd come to the theater to see.

It wasn't announced at the time, but later I found out
that my brother and his partner Yuuki came in ninth. Out of
sixty duos, that didn't seem half bad. "Pretty good!" I messaged him on LINE, but he didn't respond, so it must not
have been pretty good to him. The winners of the contest
got the chance to perform their material on the next rank's
stage.

After the show, I had tea with Natsumoto. *We see each other every day*, I thought, but he didn't seem to think that was too much, so I didn't say it.

"How did Masa's show go?"

"Mmm," I said. I thought I would come up with an answer while I hesitated, but I wasn't sure how to explain their act. It seemed cruel to only mention part of it, and I felt like it would come off as more critical of Yuuki and my brother than I had felt at the time.

"Their bit was about, like, 'compliance' and 'fuck political correctness,'" I said. "Like, 'I'm a feminist, so I hit girls same as guys'—"

"*Hya-heh-heh!*"

"Huh?"

"*Ha-hya-heh-heh!*"

*So you think that's funny?* I thought. *I wanted you to* yikes *with me.*

That part went over best in the theater, too. Yuuki and my brother had to pause for a couple of seconds, the laugh was so big. I figured we were at a comedy venue, and people were in the mood to laugh, but here was Natsumoto cracking up.

In the theater, and at this moment, too, I felt like I would turn into a ghost amid the laughter. I felt like I was the only one not laughing, like because I couldn't find it funny, I was the only one not part of the club.

I had felt so helpless. I tried to force the corners of my mouth to raise in a smile, but I was scared, and I scowled at my brother from the audience. Even though it wouldn't reach him. I didn't laugh, so at least I wouldn't disappear from myself. I scowled at Natsumoto. From this distance, I was sure it would work.

"What?" said Natsumoto. "Isn't it funny?"

"No, it's not." I did my best not to smile politely.

"You don't think so? *Hya-heh.*" Yet he evaded my point, laughing off his reaction.

But that was all. I didn't have the energy to tell him our morals weren't a match. I thought it would be a pain in the ass to continue talking about this with him. I was tired. Being exhausted from simply living, from just doing my job and having relationships with other people, was enough of a reason to do nothing. I hated myself, but my anger in that direction didn't last.

While Natsumoto went to the bathroom, I imagined the texture of the towel I had put over my head the previous day. I recalled my dark field of vision and how it was difficult to breathe. Right now, I have the towel from home on my head; I'm a ghost. The laughter doesn't make me disappear; I disappear of my own volition, and that calms me down. We used to play pretend together. Both of us became something else. Who was my brother when he was saying, "I wanna try out some material. Can I practice on you?" Whose words were those? No matter what expression I made, it wouldn't reach him; I would walk around and my ghost self would make him laugh. And that laugh? What were the laughs I got from my brother, my friends, my significant others?

When I tried to think about it, a sudden pressure weighed on my head, so I left some money on the table, went home, and tried to raise the corners of my mouth. "Ha, *hahahahaha-hahaha.*" All alone, I had no trouble laughing. I didn't have to worry about anyone or anything. I didn't have to categorize it. If I misunderstood my own laughter, it wouldn't be a problem. How fun it would be if I could laugh the whole two hours until bedtime. *My brain would have a blast—it would be great,* I thought. Wanting to forget the events of the day, I LINE'd my brother, "Nice job." I asked what place they got and said, "Pretty good!" As we chatted, I searched the name of their duo on Twitter. Among the positive comments ("OMG." "Dead." "Edgy as usual, lolol."), someone had written, "I was so scared I froze up." I was sure my brother and Yuuki were reading these, too.

What would they talk about when they saw this comment? Or maybe they wouldn't talk? I didn't ask but just laughed louder. I had never left without saying anything before, so the messages from Natsumoto were piling up. It was as if my laughter was growing with the stress of the rising notification number.

My favorite act had been the one where a guy was like, "I

like pickled plums and fried rice, so I want to make pickled-plum fried rice." By the end, he and his partner were making pickled-plum Ryuichi Sakamoto. I forgot all the funny things they said to get to that point until only my brother and his partner's jokes remained. The pickled-plum routine hadn't been uploaded yet—there were only chitchat and game streams—but I fell asleep listening to their YouTube channel.

1,004.

That was how many unread LINE messages I had when I woke up. Two from my brother, seven from my co-worker group, and 995 from Natsumoto.

My brother said they would do their best to make it big. And after that he sent a flexing-arm sticker. I thought it'd be more of a burden not to look, so I read Natsumoto's messages. His worries gradually turned to anger. By around number eight hundred, they were threats. "You better watch yourself—you can go to hell for all I care."

Imagining an emotionally unstable Natsumoto writing 995 messages made me laugh—because I realized he was probably nuts. Rather than feeling scared, I felt superior or, like, invigorated by realizing that he was nuts and not feeling guilty about that at all.

I turned off notifications from him and decided not to contact him again.

I changed my sphere of activity. I changed my route to

work and which restaurants I went to. When I got pissed wondering why I had to go to all that trouble, I bought tasty food at the department store. Every four days, I bought a pack of pickled plums and ate them both at work and at home. When a co-worker asked, "You're hooked, huh?" I answered, "I guess they're sort of a good-luck charm." "Huh, is that right." Even I was a little surprised. When I searched the duo I had liked, they didn't seem to have any solo shows coming up, so I went to the theater to see their act. It felt great to be able to find their jokes funny without any dissonance from ethical issues or discrimination. Could I bring them pickled plums as a gift? As I browsed a wide selection of pickled plums from around the country, I thought, *Well, just 'cause they mention them in their act doesn't mean they like them*, and it was then that a twisted reflection appeared in the showcase.

It was Yuuki; I recognized him from the back of his head. There aren't many other people who have a short, blond mohawk. He was looking at the chirimen sansho stand across the aisle and hadn't noticed me yet. *I wish I hadn't noticed him, either*, I thought—his head became a wave and rocked—and, *What'll I do if he asks me for my impressions of the show the other day?* But he wasn't a bad kid, so I said hi.

"Masa's sister," he said. "Whatcha doing here?"

He had been friends with my brother since their college days and had visited our family's house any number of times. He was briefly in the same seminar as Natsumoto, and on a few occasions, the three or four of us had gone drinking. Yuuki cried at the photo of our dead dog, and even went with me to visit the grave. Yeah, I wish he had been a bad kid. A good kid performing that sort of material made me feel even more awkward. But who was I to say anything?

"Just picking up some pickled plums. You like chirimen sansho, Yuuki?" I replied. *After a bit of small talk, I'll tell him that joke freaked me out. I'm going to say, "That joke freaked me out."* I chanted in my head to prep.

"Oh, I think my mom is hooked on them. Maybe I should send her some."

"Aw, that's nice of you."

"Nah, I'm not nice."

"Great weather we're having, huh?" I changed the subject.

"I guess so?"

I looked overhead. We were in the basement of a department store; my small talk had failed.

"That joke . . ."

"Huh?"

". . . freaked me out. Like, how can I explain . . . it's not like you were laughing at that stuff, right?"

"Are you talking about our act? Which performance?"

"You know, at the joke battle."

"Hmm?" He looked up at a diagonal as if scratching his brain with his eyeballs, rolling them back until only the whites showed while trying to remember. I added that they had placed ninth.

"Oh, right, right. The joke battle. But people like that kind of thing. It's a live show, not TV."

Yuuki laughed and said that it was just the business. He said he felt weird about that sort of material going over well, too, so I told him, "It must be rough," as the stress made my heart constrict, and before I knew it, I was buying enough pickled plums that I needed to pay in multiple credit card installments.

I passed them out at every year-end party I went to that year, to the point where pickled plums and I became inseparable in people's minds. *Maybe I shouldn't have given you any, then*, I thought, but I never said it to anyone's face. *I'm just as inconsistent and passive as anyone*, I thought, but I guess it really is just how people are, trying to keep the situation comfortable.

"I saw your brother on TV," my boss said to me at the company party. The previous night on one of those late shows where midcareer comedians introduced young up-and-comers, they had done an act about an ideal girlfriend. The joke about how no matter what route he took imagining his girlfriend, he ended up with an artisanal soba noodle maker got me laughing, too.

*How much do you make on a show like that? It's great that he's able to do what he likes.* Even though I'm not my brother,

I ended up getting life advice. I squeezed my hand towel, thinking of it as the bath towel at my parents' place. With it on my head, I'm a ghost, and in actuality, these people were talking at me for their own satisfaction without caring about my reply at all. *You're just talking to something transparent.*

My brother and Yuuki probably got even more comments. At New Year's he came home after all the relatives had gotten together. And he brought Natsumoto.

At the time, I was sleeping under the heated table in the living room. A tap on my shoulder woke me up, and it was Natsumoto's face in front of me; he touched my nose.

"I was so worried. Masa says you're doing well? I'm happy to see you. Phew," he said—he even had tears in his eyes.

I sensed my heart starting to feel that maybe he wasn't such a nutcase, which was confusing. I didn't want to feel so conflicted about someone who would write LINE messages like the ones he had. Unsure what to do, unsure what I wanted to do, I groaned in a half-asleep way, as if I hadn't realized it was him, and closed my eyes.

"Oh, I guess you're asleep." He laughed and then went to go help my parents wash the dishes. After he left, I would tell my brother that the joke freaked me out.

As I was pretending to be asleep, it seems I actually drifted off. When I opened my eyes, it was evening, and from the living room window, I could see my whole family plus Natsumoto out in the yard smoking. The smoke hanging in the air made everything hazy, like a dream. I could hear them laughing. Then just Natsumoto noticed me and smiled. I wished night would hurry up and come already. Once it was dark, I wouldn't be able to see outside, only my reflection in the window.

Natsumoto opened his mouth and was saying something to me.

*What?* I mouthed back. *Huh? What are you talking about? Dumbass. Shut up. Eww. The fuck.*

Having managed to say all those things and satisfy my desire to hurt him without actually hurting him, I was so happy that I smiled—but how about him? My brother and parents, looking on, we were probably all interpreting it in different ways. Once night fell, I had fun continuing that game with myself, and I wanted to put a bath towel over the whole period of time.

# HELLO, THANK YOU, EVERYTHING'S FINE

My house stands on a precipitous cliff. "Why?" I asked. "It just does," said Mom and Dad.

"What do you think?" I asked my big brother. "Why do we live on this cliff?"

"Why? We just do," he said.

"That isn't even an answer."

"Shush."

*We just do*, he grumbled.

We were in his room. The lights weren't on, so his face was illuminated by the glow of his computer screen. *Hell, heaven, hell, heaven*—the light changed like it was playing a game, in a rhythm that was impossible to predict.

"You're gonna ruin your eyes." He was crouched on his chair with both knees up wearing a black hoodie with the hood on. "You look like a hacker."

"Shush." He took the hood off. He must have felt like he looked like a hacker, too. He was typing something. Since this house stands on a precipitous cliff, we can't get internet service, but whenever I ask what he's doing on his computer, he says, *Communicating*. "The circuit is so unstable." Each time the color of the screen changed, the color of my brother's cheeks did, too.

"Dinner's ready!" Mom called from the hallway.

"Okay!" I said, and my brother said nothing.

I went to the living room and got a serving of food to take to my brother.

"I'm leaving yours here."

He didn't answer, and he was wearing his hood again, so I couldn't see his expression. "You can't even look at me?" I shrugged at the posters of Detective Conan, Inuyasha, and Lum hanging on the walls.

When I got back to the living room, Mom said, "Thanks, Marumi."

I'm the only one in the family allowed in my brother's room. I don't know why he stopped going to school. Mom and Dad know the reason, and when I sometimes hear them arguing at night in their bedroom, I assume it's about him.

So we were all surprised when he said he wanted to have a birthday party. It happened at breakfast, so we were already in shock because he only ever came out of his room at night. When he said, "Morning," Dad approached and clapped him on the shoulder.

"What's gotten into you, 'ey?" Dad said. I held my breath. The way he was acting was more than enough to scare my brother off.

"It's my birthday next week, right?"

"Sure is. What do you want? You can have anything you like."

"I don't need any presents. But I want to invite—"

"Invite?"

"Yeah, I want to invite my friends. For a party."

I swiveled my head like a Lego block to look at Mom. *Is he serious? This isn't a dream?* I had no idea he had friends.

With that, my brother went back to his room. He stayed holed up as usual until his birthday, but Mom, Dad, and I were thrilled. We gossiped about what kind of friends he might have. Dad's voice was so loud my brother might have heard him. Mom started cooking three days ahead of time and ordered a cake. On the day of, Dad left early in the morning to pick the cake up in the town at the foot of the mountain.

"I'm going to go pick up my friends," said my brother. Him leaving the house was enough to make Mom emotional. Even after he moved out of sight, she continued waving her hand in such a huge arc she was practically drawing circles.

Mom and I decided to decorate the house before he came back.

"I wonder what his friends are like."

"Who knows?"

"What kind of people are you hoping for, Marumi?"

"Mmm, I dunno."

I made a bunch of origami links, and Mom connected them into a chain and hung it on the wall. After that, we folded paper cranes and stationed them all around the house.

"I wonder if there are any girls. What'll I do if he has a girlfriend? Hey, have you noticed anything different about him lately?"

"Not really. He's always on his computer."

"Ohh. So he must have met them through the computer."

"Even though he's offline?"

"What's 'offline'? I'm sure he met them through his computer. He's got a knack for it."

"Uh . . . urgh." I was suddenly stressed. If I said I wanted to have friends over, I was sure they would talk about me when I wasn't around just like how Mom and I were talking about my brother.

"What's wrong?"

"Nothing."

My brother and his friends arrived before Dad returned. The doorbell rang, so Mom and I rushed to answer. My brother was standing there.

"Let me introduce my friends. This is Honda, that's Edmond, and Tatsuya and Kazuya are twins."

There was no one next to him. I thought they might be hiding behind him, so I walked around to see. He said again,

"This is Honda, that's Edmond, and Tatsuya and Kazuya are twins."

"O-oh!" said Mom. "Nice to meet you all." She put a hand on my back. "Come on now, say hello," she said to me.

With tears in my eyes, I said, "I'm Marumi, his little sister. Thanks for always hanging out with my brother."

My brother slipped between us and headed for the living room. The origami chain was hung at a height that meant it would sway when someone passed by, but it only reacted to my brother. I blew to move it. I thought, *It's like someone else is there.* If only thinking that would make me feel like it was true.

"Mom, we're hungry," he said.

"Huh? O-oh!" said Mom. "I'll go warm up some food. One minute."

Mom seemed glad for an excuse to hole up in the kitchen. I stood at the border between the living room and the hallway and then ran to my room before my eyes met my brother's. I closed the door in such a way that it didn't make a noise. There was no lock, and I didn't think one door was enough of a barrier, so I went out onto the balcony. A wind blew up from below the cliff, flipping my hair up off my forehead, and I was volcano shaped.

*I need to calm down. Relaaaax.* As I was breathing deeply on the balcony, a door opened. I knew it was my brother from the smell of his hair product that I could never get used to.

"If you wanna smoke, you can do it out here," he said to someone. The balcony looking off the cliff was connected to both of our rooms, so it was a space we shared. "You can keep my sister company," he said, returning through my room for some reason instead of his own.

Someone was standing next to me, but I couldn't see him.

"Umm, what was your name again?" I said as I recalled the names of my brother's friends.

"Kazuya," I said.

"Okay. So what should I call you?"

"Kazuya is fine," I said. The back of my head was hyper-aware of my brother sitting on my bed watching me.

"What should I call you?" Kazuya-me said.

"Whatever works. My family calls me Marumi."

"How about your friends?"

"My friends . . ." I had to think about it. I didn't have any friends. A brown bird landed on the outdoor AC unit. "K-K-Kotori, they call me Kotori."

"Huh. Kotori," said Kazuya. I could feel my face getting red. I rushed to explain.

"Sorry. That's a lie. Nobody calls me anything. The kids at school just call me by my last name like usual. There are some girls who talk to me and invite me to karaoke. I wanted to have actual conversations with them, and I wanted to go to karaoke. I wanted to go into our own little room and sing our songs and compliment each other. But I couldn't.

I turned down all the karaoke invitations because of this house. I think if we got to be friends, the girls would say they wanted to come over—because not too many people live in a house on a precipitous cliff. I'd say, 'Well, I don't think it's that interesting,' but my expression wouldn't deny their request. On the contrary, it might even seem like I was smiling a bit. They'd take that as an okay and climb up the mountain with me. It's a rough trek for elementary schoolers, but they'd be considerate and only complain in quiet voices I wouldn't be able to hear from up ahead.

"But then we'd have almost made it to the peak. They'll take a bunch of pictures of the house standing on the precipitous cliff. We'll take a selfie. I've never been so close to friends like this or taken a picture with them, so I can't keep the corners of my mouth still. When I go to say we should retake it because I looked bad, they're already inside the house. They head straight for this balcony. It has the best view of anywhere in the house, and they want to really taste the fact that they've come to a house standing on a precipitous cliff. And then what do you think happens? When we all flock to one place? Right, all our body weight is in one spot. The house loses its balance, and like a gag in an old movie, it tumbles roof-first off the cliff."

I crouched down and covered my face with my hands.

"Are you okay?" Kazuya asked.

"Sorry. I rambled. That was probably weird."

"Not at all. You have a rich imagination."

"What's that supposed to mean? It's not good for anything."

"You don't think so? I disagree."

"Then what's it good for? Specifically."

Kazuya was about to say something, but no matter what he said, he wouldn't be able to express what he really thought, so he decided not to say anything—is what his smile said. "You try thinking about it, Kotori," he said, bopping me on the head as he went into the house.

When I went back to the living room, I was feeling better, so I mouthed, *Thank you*, to Kazuya. He smiled. It was as if we had some kind of wonderful secret between us.

"Marumi, your food's getting cold."

"This rice ball is delicious. You're a great cook," said Edmond-Mom.

"'*Matsushima! / Ah, Matsushima / Matsushima!*' is the way you greet someone named Matsushima," said Honda-my brother.

We were playing a game. A game where you come up with fake set phrases. It got popular at my school the year before last. The boy band V6 had played it on TV, during their "Let's go to school!" special. My brother remembered me saying there was this popular game for two whole years; he must have always wanted to try it.

"My condolences. I'm terribly sorry. I'll be sure to make

the deadline. I'm currently having a merry time at Abeno Harukas," said Honda-my brother. "That's a single continuous set phrase."

"It's beautiful," said my brother.

"Wow, that's complicated," I said.

"My condolences?" said Mom.

"You try saying it, too, Marumi. 'My condolences.'"

"M-m-my com—" I stuttered.

"Nice and slow. Relax. There's no rush," said Tatsuya-my brother.

*Relaaaax.*

"My condolences." I did it. "I'm terribly? Sorry. I'll be sure to"—*Wow, I'm doing it!*—"Make the deadline. I'm c-c-currend—" Ugh!

That was when my dad, who had gone down the mountain to pick up the cake, returned.

"His friends aren't here yet?" he said as he came into the living room. With that single comment, we all fell silent.

"Um, they went to the bathroom," Mom said. She turned so the back of her head was facing my brother.

"All together?" Dad asked.

"Yes, all together." Her voice was so faint you could hardly hear it. "Right, Marumi?"

I nodded. I bobbled my face up and down. Dandruff floated down onto the oil that had seeped out of the fried chicken.

"But they're all here," said my brother. "They're right here." He looked Mom in the face, and then me. "Right, guys?"

Mom and I averted our eyes and plugged our mouths with chicken.

"What's going on here?" said Dad.

"Nice to meet you! I'm Honda," said my brother. "I'm Tatsuya," he said. He looked at our mom. He gestured with his chin for her to go.

". . . I'm Edmond," she said. It was my turn.

"I'm Kazuya."

"Tatsuya and Kazuya are twins," said my brother. "We were all just playing this set phrases ga—"

"Whoa, hold on," said Dad. "Are you all right? Hey, is everything okay?"

My brother didn't answer. He just stared Dad down. *He's so strong*, I thought. I was proud of him.

"Everything's fine," I said. I groped for Mom's hand under the table. She squeezed mine. "He's fine."

"What's fine, exactly?" said Dad. "I mean . . ."

He went to point a circle around the table, but his arm fell limply before even completing half of the loop. The table was set for four people besides our family, and the food on every plate was half-eaten. Dad put a hand to his forehead. When he was at a loss, he had this habit of sliding that hand down to his chin and sighing, so right as his hand was covering his eyes, I chomped into a piece of vinegar seaweed each from Kazuya's and Tatsuya's plates, and put them back. When Dad removed his hand from his chin and sighed, I said, "Kazuya and Tatsuya say the vinegar seaweed is tasty, Mom."

She flinched but then said, "Thanks."

"You're welcome," said Honda-my brother. "Oops, that was a real set phr—"

Before my brother could finish, Dad banged on the table. A plate fell to the floor and broke.

"Get a grip!" Dad screamed and grabbed my brother by the collar. "Why are you like this?!" Then in a much quieter voice, a voice that sounded like this argument was taking a toll on him, he said, "Why can't you just be normal?"

I squeezed Mom's hand hard under the table. My brother didn't say anything back to our dad. He just kept looking him straight in the eye.

"Hey, let's do this over," said Dad. "You don't have any friends. Let's redo your birthday party as just a family thing."

Dad crouched down to pick up the cake box he had set on the floor, and my brother pushed him. Dad face-planted into the floor, and the cake was smooshed from his chest to his belly button. The cake had been shaped like Mt. Fuji, but now our volcano was squashed.

My brother went flying out of the living room. I went after him, and once Mom helped Dad up, they followed. In my brother's room, a light like the sound of a man coughing up phlegm, like water going down a drain, like an omen, like hell, was coming out of his computer, which was blinking at a high speed that separated the light of his room from us.

"What is this? What are you doing with your computer?" I asked.

"I told you: communicating," he said. He went onto the balcony.

Dad came in and said, "Don't!" to my brother.

"Huh?" said my brother. "Oh, I see. You thought I was going to jump."

We all went onto the balcony. We put our weight on it. I wish the house really would have started leaning like a gag in an old movie. That would have meant my brother's friends actually existed. The house would tip, and we would just barely escape with our lives. Shoulders heaving, we'd turn around to see the house tumbling off the cliff, already starting to collapse into bits. We'd be overwhelmed by it. The crisis would make living between my brother and our dad seem like no big deal. We'd probably all exchange glances and laugh. *What do we do now?* we'd wonder, on the verge of tears. If our house really collapsed, I think we'd be able to start over. I went next to my brother on the balcony and jumped up and down. "Fall down!" I yelled. Dad grabbed me, and my tears fell on his arms. Until they ran to his elbows, I kept jumping.

After that my brother holed up in his room again. I was the only one allowed in his room, and he never showed his face to Dad.

First it was his mouth.

"Marumi," he said.

"What?" I looked up. I had been lying in his room writing a novel.

"Put some tape over my mouth."

"Why? Why would I put tape over your mouth?"

"That doesn't matter."

"You can tape your own mouth up."

"I'm busy." He was doing something on his computer. I sighed.

"Fine. How do you want it?"

"In an X."

I ripped off two pieces of masking tape with diagonal green and white strips and stuck them over my brother's mouth in an X.

"You look like Miffy. It doesn't hurt?"

He shook his head.

"But hey, why are you taping your mouth shut? If you get a stuffy nose, you'll suffocate."

He didn't answer. I was annoyed.

"If you don't tell me, I'll tell Mom and Dad about this."

He swiveled his chair around to face me and took the tape off to say, "Groundwork. That's all I can say at the moment."

He put the tape back over his mouth.

"Okay. I won't tell them. But once you can say why, please tell me."

He nodded.

"Good night," I said and went back to my room.

"I got three pages done today," I said to Kazuya as I sat on my bed. Of course, I knew I was only talking to myself. After considering the comment Kazuya made about my imagination that day on the balcony, I decided to write a novel.

"In this town, there's a family just like ours, and they live in a house just like this one. The foundation is sturdy, so no matter how many people go inside, it'll never tip. So my brother's friends, and mine, always come over to hang out. You're there, and Tatsuya, Edmond, Honda. Even Mitsuru Adachi is there. The kids from school are there, and my friends and my brother's friends all get along. My brother still doesn't come out of his room, but my parents don't get annoyed about it. And we have internet service, so we can communicate through screens. That's what I wrote so far. I think it's a really great story. But I'm the only one who isn't in it. My friends and you guys talk to me, but I can't see myself while I'm writing. And you know, somehow that's a relief."

I covered my face with my hands. I thought tears were going to come out, but nothing did.

"I wonder what my brother was doing back there. Do you know, Kazuya?"

"No idea," Kazuya-me said. *Yeah, I guess you wouldn't,* I thought. "Want to sneak a peek?"

I went out to the balcony and looked into my brother's room. The computer was still flashing, and when it lit up, an orangey, pee-colored glow illuminated his room.

My brother was leaving his chair to go to bed. He sat on his futon, stretched out one leg after the other; as he was lying back, he put in first his left earplug and then the right. They were shaped like bullets, but they were neither bullets nor real earplugs. He was using tape shaped to fit in his ear holes. Then he bent one knee so it looked like his leg had been amputated. With a roll of tape he took from under his arm, he made a loop around his shin and thigh. Then he taped the other leg up the same way. When his T-shirt slipped up, he stuck a big masking-tape X over his stomach. His mouth was still blocked off. The color from his computer disappeared, and the room went dark. Even once he was just a silhouette, he kept rustling around, but after a while, he stopped. The balcony window was locked, and the door to his room was locked. I thought about knocking, but I couldn't make any noise that would wake up our parents. I wanted to keep my promise not to tell them.

In the morning before I went to school, I knocked on my brother's door.

"Morning." He opened the door. His eyes were bloodshot. There was no tape anywhere on his body.

"What were you doing yesterday? In the middle of the night."

"You were watching?"

"What were you doing?"

"I said I would tell you when I could, didn't I?"

"It's nothing dangerous, right?"

"You're going to be late for school."

"Tell me it's nothing dangerous."

The door closed in my face, and my hair swayed. I heard his voice from the other side.

"I'm fine."

Every day from then on, my brother blocked off his body with tape. He said he was fine. All I could do was watch through the balcony window.

Since he couldn't love my brother, our dad gave me lots of attention. He even bought me new clothes whenever I had a parents' observation day at school. It seemed like he wanted me to wear pink frills, or almost like a wedding dress or something, but I always asked for a sweatshirt. On parents' observation day, I imitated my brother and put my hood up.

"Marumi, Marumi," he whispered from the back of the room where he was with the other guardians. "Five! It's five!"

During math class, he gave me the answer. He opened his palm and then closed it, opened it and closed it, repeating this with a huge smile and taking a step forward with each opening.

I didn't like the way he would get so childish. He didn't seem to be thinking about anything at all as he scattered his love around, and from that same place in his heart, he hurt my brother. But he was popular with the kids at school. Kuzuha wrote in her notebook, "Your dad is so cute, Myoga-saki," and showed it to me.

"I didn't know how to respond, so it ended up looking like I ignored her," I told my brother at home, but he had tape earplugs in, so he couldn't hear me. Recently he had started blocking off his body during the day, too. He was balled up on his chair staring at his computer—though his hands were bound, and his eyes had tape over them, so you couldn't really say he was looking at it. He seemed to be waiting for something. His body, along with his chair, changed directions so he was looking straight at me. All I could do was shift my eyeballs away and laugh, "*Ha-ha-ha.*" Not that anything was funny. I was thinking how I wished it could all just be a joke.

—Hello. Nice to meet you.

Suddenly I heard a voice. A voice exactly like my brother's came out of his computer. I was shocked. "Did you program it to do that?" He didn't answer. To prove I wasn't afraid, I said, "H-hello!"

—I like that energy. How's the novel coming?

"Uh, okay."

—Why a novel, anyhow?

"I mean, because it's something I can make all by myself," I said. "And writing is free. No need to worry about money. Money's important, you know. And because it's my own world. A world where I can feel safe. Everyone will read it and turn it into their own memory. That is, my world will be implanted in their heads. In the future I'll win the Cosmic Nobel Pulitzer Ultra Prize for Literature, my novel will be translated into all sorts of languages, and all sorts of people from space will turn my world into memories. And then people will start to act like the characters in my book—because my book is powerful. The memories will be powerful. Everyone will become an inhabitant of my world. Just as I planned. There won't be any more murders. And all the heartbreaking diseases will disappear. I'll feel safe. Everyone'll feel safe. You'll be able to feel safe, too."

Tears filled my eyes as I spoke. I waited for a little while, but the computer didn't answer. My brother remained perched on his chair, unmoving. He just stared at me. If my tears spilled out, it would be as if he'd made me cry.

I stood on my toes, held both hands out in front of my tummy like a ballerina, and spun around on one straight leg. If I twirled really fast, my brother wouldn't notice me crying. I was my own Beyblade. Crashing into the walls and furniture as I went, I left his room.

*Urp*—I almost threw up. I had spun so much I felt sick. It seemed like I had a concussion, and I ended up in bed. In hazy memories, I remember Mom and Dad taking turns nursing me. When I woke up in the middle of the night, Dad was next to me holding my hand, asleep. An incredibly peaceful face. Someone was standing across the room in the darkness.

It was my brother. He looked at me and mouthed something.

*Goodbye.*

Much later, I realized that must have been what he said.

At some point I fell asleep, and when I woke up, I felt good as new. The sun was just coming up, so it was still early. When I opened the door to go to the bathroom, my brother was standing outside my room.

"What's up?" I asked. He was leaning against the wall

and didn't move. His whole body was wrapped in tape, so he looked like a mummy. His nostrils were blocked, too. I winced and nervously removed the tape from his mouth.

He began breathing through his mouth as if nothing had happened. It was so calm, it scared me.

"Marumi, the groundwork is done," he said.

"For what? What groundwork? Tell me what's actually going on."

"I'm going to go be with my friends."

"Friends? You mean like Kazuya?"

"Yeah. I'm going to where Honda, Edmond, Tatsuya, and Kazuya are."

"What does that mean?"

"They weren't here, right?"

"Uh-huh . . ."

"But they're my friends. They were nice enough to be friends with me, so I want to be with them."

"What about me?" I asked. "You don't want to be with me?"

"You can talk to Kazuya, can't you? So it's okay. Will you talk to me, too?"

I tried to take the tape off of his eyes. I wanted him to look at me. I found the edges of the tape with my fingernails and peeled it off, but the eyes and skin the tape should have been outlining were missing.

"What the . . . ?"

I took all the tape off. Arms, legs, chest, neck, hair—they were all gone. He was empty. Only the mouth, only my brother's mouth remained where it was. But even that began to fade. Before his mouth disappeared and I couldn't see him at all anymore, he said, "You don't have to worry. Everything's fine."

In his room, the computer screen changed at irregular intervals to colors I didn't know the names of. *Heaven, hell, heaven, hell*. Then, as I stared at it, it went back, and nothing else happened. I picked up the computer. I tried to smash it into the floor, but when it occurred to me that this thing had spent more time with my brother than I had, I couldn't let it go. So when I swung my arms down, the momentum carried me, and I sank to the floor along with the computer. There was a mirror next to the door, so when I turned around, I could see the tape I swore I had just peeled off my brother forming his outline.

My eyes opened. Apparently I had fallen asleep in my brother's room. He wasn't there, and the lump of tape wasn't in the hall, either. When I went to the living room, my brother was there. He was talking with Mom and Dad. "Oh, hey, Marumi!" Dad said. He seemed happy.

"Morning," my brother said. I approached that brother, and as I passed, I poked the back of his hand. The brother smiled at me. I went to the kitchen and opened the garbage can. No tape. A shadow fell over me, and when I turned around, my brother was standing there. He was looking down at me. "Who are you?" I asked. The brother laid his pointer finger against his lips. He was telling me to be quiet, but I said, "Who are you?!" He kept smiling.

I decided to keep an eye on that brother. When he went back to his room, I hid behind the outdoor AC unit and observed him.

The brother was talking to someone all alone.

"Yeah, I'm okay. I'm not really used to it yet, but how are you?" I could hear him say through the window.

"Uh-huh . . . uh-huh. I see. Yeah . . . Mom and Dad are good." As the brother talked, he kept smacking his body as if there were mosquitos or something.

"Marumi?" he said. "Marumi is actually watching me right now."

His head swiveled like a twisting tree to look at me. He opened the balcony window. "Evening," he said. "Aren't you cold? Come on in."

"I'm fine here," I said. When I looked away from him, I noticed some tape lying around. "Who are you? The tape, I guess? Did you eat my brother?"

"Did I eat your brother?" he repeated. Then he laughed. He held his stomach and laughed. The top of his head was pointed at me, and I could see some tape stuck to the whorl of his hair. I reached for it. Just as I was going to pull it off, he grabbed my hand.

"Oh no. That's what happens when I lose focus." The brother straightened up and trembled. Then he bent over to show me the top of his head. There was no tape anymore. "So what were you doing?"

"Nothing."

"Hmm. He's waiting for you."

"Waiting?"

"He told you to talk to him, didn't he? Your brother. We were just chatting. Do you want to say hi?" Suddenly the brother's face changed. It was like a momentary ray of darkness. That brother had my brother's face, but I closed my eyes, and when they opened, my brother had my brother's face.

"Is it you?"

He nodded.

"What did you do? Why did this happen?"

"I can't stay long," he said. "My friends are calling me."

"Hey, do you . . . do you like us? Me and Mom and Dad."

"Yeah," he answered immediately. But it took a long time for the next words to come. "I don't really understand love, but I think it must be something like that. I like you in a loving way, which is why I could move away."

I hung my head. I could sense that he was speaking positively, so I wanted to smile, not cry. I yanked the corners of my mouth up and faced him, but my brother had already turned into the other brother.

"Sorry. He's already gone," that brother said. He had flaps of tape curling off his face like an animal's whiskers.

"I see," I said. "Thank you."

"Great. Well, good night."

"Good night." Before going back to my room, I turned around and said, "Is it fun for you here with us?"

"Yeah, it's fun. And I don't intend to stay forever, either." He poked his cheek. "I mean, look at me." When he touched his cheek, the tape turned to skin. But another strip immediately curled up, and we both laughed.

"Next week is my birthday, so please celebrate with me."

My friends were coming over for my birthday, too. It was my first time inviting anyone over. Kuzuha, Mizore, Kikka, Haori, Uta, Musubi, Riku, Meru, Eimi, and Neon were coming over. To celebrate my birthday.

When I made up my mind to invite them, everyone was happy. The only one who thought I didn't have any friends was me.

I understood how my brother felt about the importance of friends. But someday we would part ways, wouldn't we? We'd graduate, or move, or decide other friends were more important. Maybe my brother hated the thought of that, and that's why he went away.

The other brother spent all day with his body tense to maintain the form of my brother for Mom and Dad. At night, he broke out in tape. At first, I helped him put the tape back inside, but even though he thanked me, it seemed like he was stressed from the effort, so I said, "You can just be the tape. You're fine as you are." He thanked me again. I had no idea where on the person-shaped lump of tape his voice was coming from.

"Well, I'm leaving tomorrow," the tape brother said.

The next day was my birthday.

Kuzuha and the other girls came over, and we ate cake and fried chicken. As we were playing the pretend set phrases game, the tape brother left his seat. "Hey!" I said, and went after him. Perhaps remembering what had happened on my brother's birthday, Mom and Dad followed.

We went into the yard. "What's going on?" Dad asked, out of breath.

"It's nothing. Everything's fine," said the tape brother. "Everything's fine," he repeated like a curse.

Mom remained silent as if she knew everything. For a time, all we could hear were the sounds of the mountain and Dad catching his breath.

Then we heard Kuzuha and the others inside the house.

"Marumiiiiiiii!"

"Yeahhhhhhh?"

"We'll be on the balconyyyyyyyyy!"

"What?! No!" I said, but they couldn't hear me. "This is bad. The house is going to tip. All ten of them are going onto the balcony," I said to Mom and Dad.

"No, it's not built so shoddily as that," said Mom.

"But! But!" I jumped up and down.

"You're overreacting," said Dad, but just then the house creaked.

"See?!" I said, and Mom and Dad exchanged glances. We dashed toward the house.

When I turned around, the other brother was just standing there. I went back and took his hand. "You, too, bro!" I tried to run with him, but his hand had turned into tape. I had to let go so it wouldn't rip off.

"I'm leaving. This body isn't going to hold up."

"No . . ."

"It's okay," he said. "They're already on their way. Your brother, and his friends."

"What are you two doing? Get over here!" Dad shouted from the house's entrance. Mom was headed to the back of the house, shouting at Kuzuha and the others to regain the balance. Next to her, my brother and his friends were trying to stop the house from tipping. I couldn't see them, but I could.

"Let's go!" I said to the other brother.

"I don't weigh anything. I'll be useless. Just existing as your brother's body is taking all my energy."

"Let's go!" I said. "We have to save everyone. It'll be happy. We'll be happy! Let's have one last thrill all together!"

I ran with him toward the house. His tape fluttered in the wind, and as he began to blow away, it glittered in the sun. *Once my friends are safe, I'll make sure to tell my brother: See you soon.*

# A NOTE FROM THE TRANSLATOR

Thank you so much for picking up *People Who Talk to Stuffed Animals Are Nice*. Ao Omae is one of the most fascinating young authors in Japan today, so I'm thrilled to have translated his English-debut collection.

Reading the titular story for the first time was an invigorating experience. I had been following Omae since his first print collection, *Kaitengusa* (Tumbleweed), and many of his early stories were fantastically surreal (i.e., the titular story in that volume is about a tumbleweed who acts in Westerns), so to read something so rooted in contemporary Japan from him was a surprise. He has since continued to capture themes and daily discourse on Twitter in Japan, even working the COVID-19 pandemic in seamlessly.

Omae's style is disarmingly simple, but then out of nowhere he will write something extremely poetic or unusual. The example that always comes to mind is the scene in "Bath Towel Visuals" when Yuuki's head *nami ni natte yureru*—"became a wave and rocked." It's a great image, given that Masa's sister is seeing the twisted reflection of his short blond mohawk slide across the showcase glass as he turns around and notices her. There's nothing complicated about the prose, but as in picture book translation, sometimes simplicity is almost harder to get across.

I'll note one more nitty-gritty translation thing before wrapping this up. The title of the final story, "Hello, Thank You, Everything's Fine" is my own reworking of the original Japanese title, *Daijōbu no aisatsu*, which literally means something like "The set phrase 'everything's fine.'" "Aisatsu" is a word used for greetings like "hello" and "nice to meet you," which you can also think of as set phrases for daily life. It's also used for the sort of short speech one might give on a formal occasion—for example, at a company dinner, the president might welcome everyone with a few words before the meal begins. The game the characters play with set phrases is what one might call a "fake aisatsu" game. Perhaps there is no better way to sign off here than with a fake aisatsu of my own: My condolences. I'm terribly sorry. I'll be sure to make the deadline. I'm currently having a merry time at Abeno Harukas.

Emily Balistrieri
February 2023

Here ends Ao Omae's
*People Who Talk to Stuffed Animals Are Nice.*

The first edition of the book was printed and
bound at Lakeside Book Company
in Harrisonburg, Virginia, June 2023.


A NOTE ON THE TYPE

The text of this novel was set in ITC Stone Serif, a
typeface designed by Sumner Stone in 1987. During
Stone's tenure as director of typography at Adobe
Systems, he took on an ambitious endeavor to create
a font superfamily that seamlessly incorporated different type styes. Striking a harmonic balance between
cap weight, stem, and proportion, ITC Stone Serif and
its superfamily members are especially effective when
used in dictionaries, language guides, and other lin-
guistic texts.

HARPERVIA

An imprint dedicated to publishing international voices,
offering readers a chance to encounter other lives and other
points of view via the language of the imagination.